So...

∞

Volume Three

Alan D. Jones

Rising Sun Group Publishing

Atlanta, GA

Alan D. Jones/Rising Sun Group Publishing
www.alandjones.com

Publisher's Note: This is a work of fiction. Names, characters, places, and incidents are a product of the author's imagination. Locales and public names are sometimes used for atmospheric purposes. Any resemblance to actual people, living or dead, or to businesses, companies, events, institutions, or locales is completely coincidental.

Book Layout © 2020 Alan D. Jones
Editing Services: Yolanda Johnson, Anika Jones & Alan Jones
Interior Page Layout & Design: Alan Jones
Front & Back Cover Design: Alan Jones

So… Volume Three / Alan D. Jones. -- 1st ed.
ISBN 978-1-7344414-1-3

Rules of Engagement. Most of these stories are serials, meaning that new "episodes" will be released with each new volume.

CONTENTS

The Prayer Eater

From the belly of the beast, one's perspective can be quite limited. Whether chewed upon or swallowed whole, the resulting darkness is the same. On that day the truths that you once held so dear, comfort you not, save one; that all shall pass this way, whether they suffer or not. In this one regard we are all the same.

As is always the case with Voodoo Priestess, she called at two in the morning. The voice on the other end of the call, asked, "Have you checked your texts?"

"Huh? No, it's two in the morning. But of course it is."

Marketing Girl, lying next to me stirred, "Who is it?"

"You know who it is." Returning my attention back to the caller, I continued, "Let me look."

"Kisha sent a message. I think she's in trouble." She answered quickly. "Apparently, she's located the Prayer Eater, and she sent the location, just in case, we didn't hear back from her." That was as close as Kisha would ever get to asking for help. Damn, Cuz.

I should note here, that within our space and the shadows in which we move, there are rumors of beings, who are more than mortal; and possess gifts well beyond anyone in our crew. In one such being, deemed the Alchemist, we've seen clear evidence of its existence, and its gifts. In fact, it seems that in some way, this Alchemist is watching over us, dropping helpful clues, every few years or so, to aid, or at least encourage us in our collective journey. Stories abounded online about the existence of the Alchemist, but for whatever reason the Alchemist had chosen to make his or herself known only to a chosen few. But with that blessing came the curse of having to accept that creatures such as the Prayer Eater existed as well.

Voodoo Priestess went on, "Kisha's at this place they used to call *Madras Plantation* down off of interstate eighty-five. She's still trying to confirm that it's actually Prayer Eater. But she's already certain, that whatever was rumored to be happening down there, is actually happening! So, maybe it's nothing, then fine, but if it's the real deal, then…"

"Yeah, got it." I turned to Marketing Girl, "Hey, babe, I have got to go. Kisha needs us."

"I'm coming too…" she replied.

I took a breath, before answering. "Do you mind sitting in the car?"

"Really?"

"Well, if things go left, who's going to call for back up?"

"Okay, okay, whatever, let's just get going."

At the time, much of the core team still lived in Atlanta, thus the old plantation was only about an hour away from our condo. I called Grimes, who lived in our building, and told him to meet us on the street. He asked why, and I told him it was Kisha. End of discussion.

With Grimes in tow, we sped down I-85 towards our destination. Of course, Grimes quizzed me all along the way. Each time I answered with some variation of "All I know is that Kisha thinks she's located the Prayer Eater."

Nearing the plantation, I could see that the field was full of cars, at least thirty of them. But per Kisha's instruction, we pulled in behind an old abandoned shack, right before reaching our destination. There I saw Roughneck's Dodge Charger and

Voodoo Priestess' rental car. Apparently, she and Kisha had been tracking the Prayer Eater, as we all had. But for whatever reason, the pair chose not to pull the rest of the team in until they'd confirmed that this thing, whatever it was, was going down.

Kisha was in the forward position keeping an eye on the house. So, once we all assembled, we followed Voodoo Priestess to Kisha's location. Hiding behind a slightly crumbled wall, Kisha debriefed us, "He's in there…" she said as she nodded her head toward the recently restored plantation. Apparently, through a series of shell companies, the Prayer Eater or his surrogates had acquired the former slave plantation. This plantation had an additional meaning for Kisha and me, in that it was also the place where our maternal ancestors were enslaved, and where my great-grandfather worked as a sharecropper.

Kisha continued on, "…and it appears that he's here to perform one of these *chosen* ceremonies, we've heard about." Kisha paused before going on, "And if what we've found out regarding these events is true, most of the guests will not leave here alive."

"So, what's the play?" Roughneck asked of his sometime paramour.

Kisha answered, "We have to disrupt this event by any means necessary."

Grimes chirped up, "Didn't our benefactor from the rafters," meaning the Alchemist, "tell us to leave this fool alone?"

Marketing Girl, who was back in our car, answered over our ear plugs, "But we have evidence that most of the kids that attend these events are never seen again. And no one knows what he's doing to these kids. Worst case, and we have to assume the worst, is that he's killing them."

Roughneck grumbled, "No, sometimes you are better off dead. At least, you're at peace then." He'd seen enough death and suffering to make that calculation.

I offered, "You know sometimes, sunshine is the best disinfectant against those who work in the shadows."

"So, what are you saying?" Grimes asked.

"I mean yeah, we try to break this up, but maybe we go in there streaming, or at least recording. Then we upload the footage exposing his evil ass. And maybe word gets around regarding what's actually happening at these things." I let that sit with the others for a moment.

"That's a good idea, cuz. Then maybe we can avoid these littler gatherings altogether. Let's do it." Kisha answered.

Walking through the rows of parked cars two by two, we closed in on the big house, quietly. Amazingly, there was no security, beyond the greeters who pointed us towards the seating area.

It was the most amazing and distressful thing I'd ever seen in my life up to that point. There he was, the Prayer Eater, in the flesh, speaking to all of those teens and young adults. He stood on a stage riser with a podium before him, and a couple of acolytes flanking him to his left and right, with a doorframe behind them, sitting right before what appeared to be a bed of coals enclosed in what looked like a four-sided plexiglass shower stall.

We entered the room mid speech, but the Prayer Eater didn't skip a beat. "You know, truth be told, modern technology has made it far easier for me to connect with my recruitment base." His *gatherers*, as he called them, hung out on nihilistic websites and Reddit threads, seeking out the vulnerable. He went on, confessing, "I seek out the hopeless like you to fill my ranks. For once you're hopeless, you're an empty vessel which I can sculpt to my needs and the needs of the cause!"

Then he slung off his cape revealing a pair of wings protruding from is shoulder blades, "As some of you knew before you arrived, the entrance you crossed to join us here, was indeed a door of no return. Either you will be transformed into something greater, or you will die here tonight." He paused again, before going on, "Thus, we must separate the wheat from the chaff." And with those words a wall of flames erupted from the bed of coals behind the doorframe on the stage.

"Yes, many of you will die. But for you who are transformed, a great and unspeakable destiny awaits you!" Then, after glancing back at the inferno, the demon turned back towards and offered with a sly smile, "Though it is said that those who worship me, fare a bit better…" After a grim chuckle, the demon's face hardened, as he pointed towards the first two rows of guests sitting in folding chairs and ordered. "Arise…!!!"

"What the hell?" Roughneck shouted as we all jumped to our feet and began pushing through the crowd towards the Prayer Eater, but the faithful resisted our movements, thinking that we were trying to jump the line.

Finally acknowledging our presence, the winged host said loudly, "…and we have some uninvited guests in the back. Do with them as you please."

Thus, before we could do much of anything, several of the young people from the front row, had stepped into the flames, screaming in agony, their ashes either rising to the exhaust fan above, or falling through the grates below.

Fighting against the throngs I screamed out, "No…!!!".

And just as I screamed, Voodoo Priestess touched me on my temples and whispered into my ear, "Let go…"

The next thing I knew, my shoulder was in the demon's chest, and I was driving him back through the rear wall of the makeshift, unholy sanctuary. When I came to my senses, I and my opponent were outside strewn in the wet Georgia grass, and I had little clue as to how I'd gotten there, even though the feeling, the loss of control, took me back to my childhood, when I was falling into the sky. And honestly, in that latter-day moment, my heart was not racing because of the demon I'd just tackled, but rather from the rush of energy coursing through me. I felt I might literally burst.

Voodoo Priestess was on my heels, and her amulet glowed as she recited one incantation after another seeking to bind the beast, even as it breathed flames of fire towards her. But somehow, she was shielded, as the flames arched around her.

Just then, Cousin Kisha entered the lawn through the hole in the rear wall that I and our opponent had just made. The Prayer Eater caught sight of her and yelled, "Gatekeeper, this is not your day!" Then as he quickly targeted a stream of fire in Kisha's direction, she dove behind one of the air conditioning compressors which lined the rear of the building, and even more incredibly, she managed to launch an arrow, as she dove, which struck the beast in its left eye.

Enraged, the beast took on his true form, doubling in size, such that he towered over us. Roughneck who was now in play, fired several shots at the demon to no avail. As he partially hid himself behind the corner of the brick side wall, he yelled to Voodoo Priestess, "Should you call up Solomon?"

Voodoo Priestess, shook her head in response, to Roughneck's request to call up the avenging wraith from the pit. "No, too many kids, too much collateral damage, once he finished with this guy, assuming that he could stop him. Plus, if I should fall, who among you could send Solomon back to the pit?"

While all of this was going on, Grimes had managed to somehow quickly find the natural gas shutoff, shutting down the incinerator inside. To his credit, Grimes seemed to know all these sort of seemingly trivial survival tips, that seemed useless, until they weren't. But shutting things down inside, led some of the young folks from inside, to wander into the line of fire outside.

Voodoo Priestess was able to stand before the Prayer Eater, which allowed us to discuss over our headsets that perhaps with her protection, Kisha could get off another arrow into the beast's other eye. But our window was small and closing for any such action, because Voodoo Priestess was clearly withering under his assault.

I offered, "Can you supercharge me again, or whatever you did? Maybe I could tackle him again?"

She yelled back, "Your heart is still racing, right? Doing that again so soon will likely kill you."

The Prayer Eater, given that name because of his ability to literally feed off of the despair of others, took a moment to stretch out his left hand, causing two portals from the pit to open, releasing shadow demons (unable to fully take form on our dimension, they appeared as shadows to the living), who immediately began chasing down the hopeless. Then the beast returned his attention to Voodoo Priestess and toasting more of his invitees, even as some of the guests, in the darkness, fell through the portals he'd just opened. All of this chaos was only making him stronger. Then, seeing Voodoo Priestess fall to one knee, I yelled "I'm willing!"

Leveraging her gift, within the blink of an eye Voodoo Priestess was standing next me, panting. And as I took a deep breath trying to calm myself, before she cranked me up again, a nearly blinding light appeared above us. It was a bluish circle which illuminated the entire plantation, which was no small feat. Not even a moment later, a silver star floated to the ground not a hundred yards from where we stood. In the next moment a shimmering blue wall surrounded the plantation.

One of the lower demons cried out, "Master...!!!"

The beast looked up, "Damnit! The Alchemist is here! And they never travel alone…" Ignoring us for the moment, and hunched, the Prayer Eater scanned the darkness all around us. He muttered, "Always two, sometimes three…" Then from the darkness, a pair of red beams cut through the night, severing the demon's left arm from its shoulder. As the demon screamed into the night, "Arghh….!!!", a portal of his own creation opened up beneath him, allowing him to slither back into the pit from which he crawled.

Then in quick succession, each of the demons the Prayer Eater left roaming the grounds was dispatched in various forms, all of which allowed our benefactors to remain far enough away from us that we could not see their faces. They moved in the darkness, with a quickness, which would have been hard to believe, had I not witnessed their deeds with my own eyes.

Then suddenly, with seemingly just a turn of the page, there was calm. In the distance, on the edge of the property, between nine o'clock and twelve, we saw three figures in the darkness. The first one, hovering in the air, stared back at us through a pair of beaming red eyes. While a second shone like a silver star and the third, floating high above the others in a blue bubble, giving off the glow which illuminated everything in various shades of blue.

Voodoo Priestess, standing next to me could only utter, "Wow…"

Then I heard another voice next to me say, "The one on the ground is the Alchemist." It was Grimes. He continued on, "Folks online say that he has a silver aura about him."

"Online?"

"Oh, you poo-poo the dark web, but they be knowing sometimes."

"Like once in a thousand times?"

"Yeah, but still when they're right, they're right."

After settling the young folks down, and making sure that none needed a ride, we began the short trek back to our own cars. Several of the survivors called the police, we didn't want to be around for that. Walking next to Voodoo Priestess, I had to ask her, "So, what did you do to me?"

"You have gifts beyond those that you use. You've always been comfortable developing your gift of knowledge, and ultimately, it is your greatest gift. But like me, you have other gifts which you suppress, for they terrify you."

"Really?"

"But your physical reaction back there, with your heart nearly bursting, tells me you're still not ready for your full destiny. But someday, I hope you will be."

Epilogue: After getting a hold of their invitation list (who uses printouts anymore, beside old, retro demons, right?), we setup of a website for those who attended the event at the Madras Plantation, which allowed them to interact with a counselor, or to connect to some in person resources. The authorities chalked up much of what was in their official reports of the incident to mass hysteria. But anyone who was there that night knew better. For on that day, the hopeless, had their unspoken prayers answered in a most unforgettable way.

Something Always Wrong.

"Noob alert, four o'clock...!!!" Grimes called out.

Grimes was certain that some bullshit was about to go down. "I've been tracking these fools online for a month. They think they can just do anything. But they gonna learn today!" Grimes had come across a group online, planning some meetup event, and he just knew that they were speaking in code for some sort of mass killing. Of course, when he first asked me to join him, I asked why didn't he take this information to the police?

His reply was revealing. "I did. I went down to the police station and showed them what I found, and you know what they said?"

"No, I don't. What did they say?"

"They had the nerve to ask me, who my doctor was, and if it was okay if they gave him a call? You believe that shit?"

I shrugged my shoulders, struggling to restrain a smile, or much worse, to burst out laughing. That was several days ago, and now here we were in the Whole Foods parking lot on Ponce, awaiting the apocalypse.

So, by this point in the story you may be asking, why in the world was I sitting there in the Whole Foods parking lot with Grimes, at seven in the morning awaiting this *terrible thing* to go down, even though he'd never specified to me exactly what we were planning to do about it? Well, once I realized that he was actually going to go through with this, I figured I had two choices. Either go with him and try to mitigate the situation or let him go alone, and then face the consequences of getting him an attorney, which I'd end up paying for (he makes decent money, but he spends every dime he gets), spending my valuable time going back and forth to the jail with said attorney and lastly having to explain to Marketing Girl why I let him get himself locked up again? Those are the kinds of conversations that men dread having with their lady or partner. Regardless of the identity, the dynamics of Monday morning quarterbacking remain the same.

As we waited, I noticed that Grimes was slouched down in his seat, as though he didn't want to be seen.

"Dude, why are you doing that? These cats don't know you from Adam."

"No, they don't, but it's not them I'm worried about. I know this girl who hangs out down here sometimes, and I'd rather not see her this morning."

"She's homeless, right?"

"See, you're wrong! She's not homeless…"

"So, she's got her own place then, I take it?"

"Well, it's not actually her place, but a mutual friend of hers and mine, is putting her up for a few days at a place around the corner."

"Dude…?"

"Look man, I've tried to play it straight, but relationships just aren't my thing. And really, I'm just cutting through the bullshit. This modern-day love thing is a battle, that takes no prisoners."

"Really?"

"Yes, without question. For better or worse, seen or unseen, everything between men and women is transactional. So, why not just cut to the chase?"

"Then why not just hire a pro?"

"Dude, what kind of man do you take me for?"

All I could do was to shake my head. Then after several moments of silence, in all sincerity I asked him, "Grimes, who hurt you?"

"Who didn't?"

"Dude?"

A moment passed, so I felt it okay to pull out my phone to check my email, without being offensive. Maybe I was wrong.

"Blerd, what you got on?"

"Shorts, a tee, and some jogging shoes."

"No, that's not what I'm asking. I'm asking *what is that you've got on?*"

"Dude..."

"Not hating, but you look like you might *possibly* be homeless."

"Homeless?"

"Or maybe even a wino... No offense to winos."

"Hey, you inserted yourself into Saturday my morning flow of jogging to the gym, working out and then running back home to Marketing Girl. But I moved everything back, just to sit here with you, waiting on what?"

"Look man, I know you're making a grip, and yet you're always raggedy and sporting some ugly ass shoes. Why? The Universe wants to know."

"These are a hundred eighty-dollar Asics running shoes."

"And they're ugly as hell… Can you take them back?"

"You know sometimes I think you invite me out to these little escapades of yours, just so you can clown me."

Grimes smiled but said nothing.

We sat there quietly for almost thirty seconds, before Grimes spoke once again, "Hey, let me ask you something?"

"Sure…"

"Have you ever considered that I might be a figment of your imagination?"

"You told me that you'd left that synthetic shit alone…"

"No, I'm serious. Like, how would you know?"

"Well, first off, I would hope that other people in my life, would tell me the truth of things."

"But what if the whole team is the product of some sort of psychotic break on your side? Like none of us really exists?"

"…Well, I've known Kisha basically all of my life. And if I was going around talking to imaginary people Kisha would…"

"No, you're right. There's no way in the eternal hell that Kisha would play along with that." Grimes paused for moment, then added, "So, what if I'm a figment of your imagination?" Then he proceeded to prod me in the shoulder.

"Dude!" I yelled as I pushed his hand away.

"I'm just wondering how any of us can be sure of what's real?"

"Look man, have you ever considered getting a dog or maybe a cat?"

"Negro, please…"

"You need something or someone to help balance your life."

"I got my plants."

"Which you smoke."

"Damn right. That's a healthy relationship in my book."

I threw in the towel.

A couple of minutes later, about four before seven, a loose assortment of folks, began to gather in front of the store waiting for the doors to open. But to Grimes credit, while it appeared there were the usual Saturday morning early risers anxiously waiting to get into Whole Foods, there were others who appeared to be setting up to film something on their various smart phones.

Grimes called his shot, "It's about to pop off!" Then he reached for the gun he kept under his seat. Quickly, he said "I'll pop the trunk and you can grab the shotgun out the trunk."

I grabbed a fist full of his jacket to slow his roll. "Dude, let's let this playout a little longer." Plus, I for one had little interest, as a black man, hauling out a fully loaded shot gun from anyone's trunk, and charging into any store with it, even in Atlanta. Seeing some of the growing crowd begin to film themselves on their phones, I activated a custom app of my own creation on my phone, to listen into the audio feed from several would be film makers. I had the feed playing in my ear, but then I switched the playback to my phone's speaker. Lowering my window, I looked up and pointed to the fancy drone filming them from high above the parking lot. "See?"

Grimes sat in silence for a moment, "They're giving shout outs to their Tic-Tok followers?" He looked puzzled for a moment. I gave him a look as I shook my head, then my realization fell upon him. "Blerd, they kept talking about Tic-Tok and using a Tic-Tok hashtag for everything they posted, so I assumed that was code for some kind of suicide bomber shit, you know?"

"Why would you assume that?"

"Dude…" Grimes threw up his hands like I should already know. Grimes' life view defaulted to the worst case. His belief is that if you always assume the worst, you'll never be disappointed. But he needed to add a rider to his social contract, that stated *you will often find yourself in random parking lots at seven in the morning, and pulling your friends into your foolishness.*

And yet, when Grimes was involved, I knew that the probability of things going left, were exponentially higher, for he is the one variable, from which he cannot escape. That day was just one of many such days. So, a moment later I looked up from my phone to see a gaggle of clowns, evil looking ones, marching from the Home Depot parking lot towards Whole Foods. Being in Atlanta, you're going to see some things, so most often you just roll with it. But as I was watching, I saw that they were carrying objects in their hands. I pointed out the window towards them, "Grimes, you see that?"

"What?"

"Down by the Home Depot."

"Oh, looks like a bunch of clowns, a bunch of clowns carrying baseball bats, mace and chains. You think those are props or the real deal?"

"I don't know, but seeing how their bodies move, when they're swinging them, I know that they have some weight to them."

Right then a second wave of realization swept across Grimes' face as he shook his head. "Oh, I know who they are. They call themselves, Payasos Locos." Loosely translated, "Crazy Ass Clowns."

"Yeah, I've heard of them. They're a vigilante group that roams the streets taking out vengeance against *capitalists* who have been reported to have mistreated their workers. But I'm amazed to see them out here doing their thing during the day!"

"Well, I might have mentioned to them something about this Tic-Tok thing going down this morning…"

"Dude!"

"Sorry, Bro. I kind of forgot. But I didn't expect them to actually show up."

"You didn't expect them to show up? I've told you before, these cats aren't just keyboard activist. They're real ones, if ever there were!" Like a certain spectrum of the progressive wing in our nation, they ain't right, but they sure as hell ain't wrong either. We needed to stop this thing from going down, but unfortunately, the Payasos Locos wouldn't know who in the hell, I or Grimes was, if we ran down the parking lot to stop them because we never share images of ourselves or our real names online.

Grimes, took out his smart phone and after a couple of clicks he shouted into his cell phone, "Abort, abort!!!".

"Dude, you think that group is online, checking their mentions right now? Bro, I think we're going to have to go over there and tell them what's up."

"But if I walk over there and give them my online name, that puts our whole team at risk."

"True. But we can't allow innocents to be hurt. That's the first law in life." Grimes shook his head, as I began to open the passenger door. "Look, we'll figure it out."

Grimes followed my lead and exited the car, just as the armed clowns strode pass Staples which was attached to Whole Foods. But as we were briskly striding to intercept the face painted would be heroes, half of the Tik-Toc creators closer to Staples took on perplexing looks as they turned from their camera in the sky. But the other Tic-Toc folks seemed to be looking back past Grimes and me, towards Ponce de Leon. So, I glanced to my right and spotted a swarm of super heroes and villains jogging in a near sprint towards the Whole Foods entrance.

Grimes stumbled as he caught a glimpse of the approaching crowd which was larger than the Clowns and Tic-Tok creators combined. "What the f…" he started to exclaim.

I grabbed Grimes' arm, "They're cos players from Dragon-Con!" then I paused a moment, "Hey weren't you down there yesterday?"

Grimes had a moment, then confessed, "Yeah, I was down there for a few minutes."

"Grimes…???" I waited a moment, for him to confess.

And then it came out, "Well, I may have mentioned something about this to a few of the fanboys and girls in the badge line with me."

I shook my head.

"Dude, I was just sharing some things I'd read online. I didn't realize that they'd actually come down here."

"Well, the good news is that now that they're here, I think seeing such a large number of folks coming at them from the other side has given the Crazy Ass Clowns a reason to pause.

…well, at least until they realize that they're all coz players carrying plastic swords and shields. But I have an idea…"

"What is…", Grimes started to ask, when he was blindsided with a punch that knocked him to the ground.

Instinctually, I raised my hand to protect my fallen friend, as my other hand reached for Grimes looking to pull him back to his feet. At that moment I took in his assailant, and saw that it was a young woman. She cursed, "Where you been, mother…", as she tried to kick my fallen teammate. "You said that you'd pay my car note and my light bill, and I ain't seen your sorry ass since…"

Ah, the lights went on in my own head. This was one of Grimes' ladies, and I had zero doubt that he promised her this and that to lure her in. Grimes had two fixations, eastern European women, and women in need. Thus, his proclivity for homeless women and women down on their financial luck. Hell, the whole reason that he lives in the same midtown high rise that I do, is to pull women. But in truth, Grimes really can't afford to live there. He does some contract work, but on the low, he has a pay-to-view site, where he dons a mask and performs certain acts on himself. By this time, he'd cut back a bit, as he realized the collective toll of these stunts on his body. And the thing is, he's really good at his legit profession, and actually, he's one of the best in his lane. But to say that he doesn't play well with others, is a vast understatement.

At this point on our journey, Grimes was forty years old, and the young lady appeared to be twenty or so. I'd told him repeatedly, that all of this was bad karma and that it would someday come back on him. And that day, Karma was collecting and her young legs were kicking his old ass.

At last, I was finally able to separate the two of them, as she continued to yell at Grimes. "I told you about my bills, the ones you said you'd pay, then you ghosted me. I got a daughter to feed, and I don't have time for your bullshit. We had and *understanding*, you said, and I counted on you doing what you promised!"

"Look babe, I just need to move some things around. I got you!"

"Bullshit! Stop with the bullshit. I can't stand broke ass…"

Grimes interrupted her "Well, you out here fighting me because I'm little late on the money, I'm *giving* you, so what does that make you???"

Why did he say that? So, she went to wind-milling her arms, before taking a boxing stance, which told me that she'd had some training in the *sweet science*, as the art of throwing hands is often called. She was no threat to me, but Grimes really can't fight (he's more of a pull out the strap kind of guy), so seeing him trying to fend off her jabs was quite entertaining. In fact, so much so, that the incident caught the attention of all three would-be war parties. Grimes and his assailant were doing a dance where Grimes, to his credit, tried to simply grab her, to somehow restraint her (meaning that at least he had sense enough not to take a swing at her). But girlfriend's bob and weave game was tight, and her right hand mighty. After getting knocked to the parking lot pavement for at least the third time, Grimes got up and took off running. His former love interest ran after him, before stopping, removing her shoe and throwing it at Grimes as he ran. The high arching toss, somehow, miraculously hit my boy square on his head, causing him to fall out face first. The collective crowd, transfixed by said events, erupted into a unified cheer impressed by the young woman's marksmanship. As the crowd celebrated, Grimes yelled out, "I've been shot…!!! Somebody call nine, one, one!!!"

The girl yelled back at him, "That's what you get, with yo punk ass! I better not find you back out on these streets until you pay me what you owe!"

Just then, my phone buzzed. It was Marketing Girl, so I answered. "Blerd, I was watching this Tic-Tok live event on my phone, when saw you, and some woman!"

"MG, that's Grimes' girl."

"When you left, I thought you were going to gym, like you do every Saturday morning, but now I see you down in front of Whole Foods caught up in some foolishness! And on top of all that you lied to me!"

"Darling, I never said that I was going to the gym. I mean, actually since you were asleep, I don't see how it would be technically possible for me to have lied to you..." Though in truth, I knew that she would have thrown a fit, if she had known that I was connecting with Grimes, about anything.

"Boy, don't play with me! You know damn well, I wouldn't have let you leave the house, if I'd had known you were meeting Grimes for anything." She said, confirming my point.

Of course, I thought to push back, with a "... if you'd get up before noon on the weekends, you could be a part of these conversations." But I have better sense than to say anything like that, so instead I offered "You're right baby..."

She said a few other things as well, but I don't recall them all. While she lectured, I thought "Of course this would be the one morning that she actually, set her alarm to see this must watch Tic Toc event." Regardless, I replied, "You're right baby...", repeatedly.

MG said a couple more things, all of which I answered with a simple, "Sho' you're right baby..."

After taking a breath, she asked, "Why are you still standing there? Go get your boy. Atlanta's finest are on the scene now, and I'm sure that he's got some outstanding warrants for something or other." She was right about that. Grimes has never paid a fine, for parking or otherwise, in his life. Plus, I'm sure that there were at least a few folks he owed on the Tik-Toc live feed, who were lacing up to come down to Whole Foods for their pound of flesh, and a bit of freshly made guac.

As the police department officers began speaking with the various parties, I reached Grimes and snatched him up by the shoulder. But after coming to a standing position, he still resisted, "Man, what are you doing, I've been shot…, shot in the head!"

"Fool, if you'd been shot in the head, you would not be talking, much less be able to walk. Let's get out of here before anyone suspects that you're Grimes." Grimes wasn't his real name, but on those digital streets, and in the context of our "Do Right" collective, he was known as Grimes. And it had been Grimes who had, perhaps unwittingly, stoked this virtual fire, into a real-life event. Reaching the car, after we had both quietly taken our seats, I asked my digital brother, "Why is it, that your problems seem to always become my problems?"

"Dude, you're looking at this all wrong. Had I not dragged you out here, who knows what would have gone down? We should be celebrating."

"Really…? Ah, aren't these cosplayers and clowns here only because of you?"

"Hmm, I see your point there. Hey, you got me. I got nothing. My bad. Hey, where can we get a slice this time of morning?"

"Really…? You just gonna… You know what, squash it. Pizza at seven in the morning? Publix frozen food section."

"Yeah, you're right about that. What about breakfast?"

"Thumbs Up?"

"That'll work. Can you spot me some cash?"

"Really? You know you need your ass beat for the way you clowned this morning?"

Grimes said nothing, but held his hands up as to frame his face and the bruises on it, suggesting that he'd already gotten his ass beaten that morning, although most of the damage was self-inflicted from when he faceplanted into the pavement after he thought he'd been shot.

I thought to myself, "This negro, here…"

Sullen Girl.

Some see fire as unforgiving, but for me, it's always been redeeming, holy, if you will. So, yes, when my day comes, cremate my black ass. ...Or so, I'd always said before. But I must make amends. Fire bracketed within ceremony is holy, but cast down by wicked hands upon the righteous, it can be outright blasphemous.

When we arrived at her Maui home, in the darkness, the embers were still smoldering. The devastation we witnessed was in stark contrast to the seemingly eternal waves crashing against the shore just across the main road as the sickled moon shone over all.

Only a month earlier she had joined us in Atlanta to assist in rescuing my former school teacher. Now, her ashes were presumed to be among the ashes blowing in the gentle night breeze. Falling to his knees beside me, Grimes cried out, "Oh baby girl..." and in his grief, he breached protocol, to, in an open space, speak her true given name into the atmosphere. Even in death, we must adhere to the code, the code that keeps us safe, as safe as possible anyway. But I allowed my brother some grace on this day.

I knew for some time that the Russian had a place here in Maui, and she knew that I knew. In fact, she once offered in passing, that I was welcome to watch her back regarding this property, her undisclosed sanctuary. She didn't have to say it twice, which was what she expected of me. So, soon after I used one of my long-range drones to drop a solar powered camera with a secured satellite uplink to watch her place. All of which she could have done, but the AI piece to recognize threats versus postal workers, was more my lane, than hers. I was honored that she trusted me so. But alas, it seemed that it had all been for naught.

Grimes asked me the most obvious question, "Why would she come here, after what went down in Atlanta. She should have been a ghost for at least six months before even thinking of returning to the states."

"I know." I offered grimly.

"And it wasn't those Entropy assholes?" Grimes asked. Let me back up a second. Suffice it to say, we were in a bit of a circular firing squad. Several state actors were on the hunt for Entropy for hacking their banking systems and stealing billions. Some of these same countries were also after the Russian for stealing state secrets and releasing them to the public. And lastly, Entropy wanted my whole team dead for the offense of returning the retirement savings they'd stolen to their victims. It was known on the dark web, that they had not let such an offense go unpunished. Before this point in our collective journey, they'd only managed to kill one team member, Money. And while we are all greatly saddened by Money's death, he'd left a path of carnage prior to connecting with my team, so he halfway expected that he might someday catch a bullet, be it from a disgruntled husband, mistress or investor. So, we thought he was safe as long as he stayed away from the scene of the crime (pretty much the entire northeastern United States), so to speak. Likewise, the Russian had spent her life fighting for the people against the powers that be, knew that her days were numbered. She knew that she was a target. But she wasn't worried about some dude with a grudge, who hit the gun range twice a year, creeping up on her. No, her enemies were far better equipped.

I answered Grimes, "No, this was state sponsored. In fact, a couple of our elected officials sanctioned it." A crawling AI routine I run online picked up some chatter regarding The Russian. The alert would have gone directly to her, just as it went to me. And still she was here when they struck. In the moment, I didn't get it. She knew they were getting close.

The lab reports confirming that it was indeed The Russian wouldn't come back for weeks, but I already knew, as I always do. I also knew that Entropy didn't know about this hit on The Russian. In fact, they didn't even know that The Russian was in Hawaii.

Grimes moaned, "I didn't even know that she lived here." I held my peace, lest I find myself lying to Grimes. I knew well that The Russian did not want Grimes knowing the location of her secret hideaway, for one very defining trait of Grimes is his inability to keep secrets. Then unprompted by me, Grimes added, "But maybe that was for the best, 'cause I would have been over here all the time."

"Yeah, you would have." I tried to smile as I nodded in agreement. Grimes was also known as someone who wasn't' very good at respecting boundaries.

Through his tears, Grimes answered "Guess, you're right about that."

"We need to get up out of here, before we draw too much attention." I realized that it would be so very uncool, if some random dude somehow got a picture of us standing there amidst charred the ruins.

But as we made our way back to the airport, I ran the events of the last forty-eight hours over and over in my mind looking for what I may have missed. What happened was clear as day to me, and yet the feeling that something wasn't right stuck with me, up to and past the point when Grimes and I parted ways. His flight was in an hour, but mine wasn't until the following day (we never flew together, for obvious reasons).

In a small village one hundred kilometers from Sklad, Sakha Republic, Russia; Circa 1988

I turn to the right and there I am, in a house with no mirrors.

I turn to my left, and my view is no clearer.

Now, it all seems like a dream.

But nothing is as it seems.

In my hotel room the questions bugged me so much that I couldn't sleep. So, I cracked open my laptop. My gift was such that what I looked for, I found. But in this instance, I wasn't even sure what question to ask. It wasn't our mission to take on state actors, as The Russian had done in her life prior to joining our team. And though it hurt like hell, we always knew that this was a possibility. And yet, my intuition implored me to keep digging, into what seemed to be an open and shut case.

Then something struck me. The Russian spoke fondly about her childhood home, near the town of Vladivostok, in western Russia and how Vancouver reminded her of home. "But a bit colder…" she would always add afterwards. Then something inside of me clicked. If she, and rightly so, hid the existence of this home from the rest of the team, then it was likely that she had another domicile somewhere that she'd kept from me. At the time, I was still doing remote contract work, so I had the flexibility to change my travel plans. I rebooked my flight home to include a couple days in Vancouver. I loved Vancouver too.

Shoulder rides, one at a time.

Side by side, nursery rhymes.

Smile like the sun, voice of thunder.

Suddenly disappeared, worlds asunder.

I landed in Vancouver as daylight broke. Grabbing a map, I spread it out before me. Though I knew I had this very special gift, these events were in the days before I fully knew what I was. So, I was left placing myself into The Russian's shoes, knowing what she liked, and knowing the city pretty well, I deduced which parts of town she would be inclined to live. Well, that's what I told myself about how I could repeatedly be right about such things. And yet, I found myself at a breakfast spot sitting across the street from a small coffee shop. Well, it wasn't just any coffee shop. See, unlike Entropy, I actually knew The Russian's real name, or at the least the one she used when living her real life. So, since she was now dead, I saw it as no invasion of privacy to hack into the retail virtual cloud, to see her buying habits. In my digging, I did find, that somehow her transaction history made it appear that she'd made "card present" purchases, against different bank credit cards, thousands of miles apart within the same hour. That seemed odd, but I dismissed it as bad reporting or legacy vendors manually processing purchases days after the fact. But regardless of those outliers, it was clear that when she was in Vancouver, this coffee shop was her Saturday morning spot.

As I sat there over my half-eaten pancakes, waiting for something to justify my being there (some clue or profound insight), my thoughts drifted back to bits and pieces of conversations that I'd shared with The Russian and her confidant, Voodoo Priestess. The two had bonded over a matter way back when, and remained close, come what may. There in the wooden acreage, somewhere in Dekalb county, Georgia, as we all parted ways, the demeanor of Voodoo Priestess when she told The Russian's goodbye, struck me funny, even in the moment and much so now, in that there was a finality to it, which seemed misplaced.

The wait person stepped over to me and asked, "Will there be anything else?"

I answered her, "A refill on the coffee and the check, if you don't mind." Then, as I turned my attention back to the coffee shop across the street, I saw a blonde-haired woman in a blue dress walking away from me and towards the café. Her stride was familiar.

Tossing my money upon the table and abandoning my new cup of hot coffee, I snatched my backpack up, and slinging it upon my shoulder, I departed the restaurant with all due haste, but not so fast as to alarm any of the patrons. Checking for oncoming cars, I crossed the street at a brisk pace.

Entering the coffee shop, my eye caught sight of the blonde-headed woman in the blue two-piece suit, with her back to me. Then my focus adjusted, and I could see clearly, that the woman sitting across from her was a dead ringer for The Russian. Then the woman in blue turned her head to take me in over her shoulder, and I saw that she too was The Russian. In that moment all of the scales fell from my eyes and everything fell into place. From the moment we encountered Entropy's assassins, with their night vision bodycams in the woods of east Atlanta, she knew. And as we parted and she and Voodoo Priestess walked away embracing one another, they both knew that the prophecy she'd spoken to The Russian years ago, was at last being fulfilled. She knew what she had to do to protect her sisters and the mission to which they'd been called.

From their table, the faces of the two remaining sisters conveyed a deep concern, but then after nodding to one another, they motioned for me to join them. Wave after wave of realization swept over me, with each step I took towards them. The depth of their commitment to each other and to avenge their father, was without limit.

Three lives, one life.

Three loves, one strife.

Three beings, one soul

Three sisters, one goal

You're Somebody Else.

"Blerd, I tell ya, you just never know, do you?" said the ubiquitous Grimes over his cell, as our train pulled away from the station.

And though he meant it in a very limited way regarding his girl, my "yeah…" reflected my more expansive existential perspective.

Often, in love, you never know for sure who is the slave and who is the master, for there is no compass of use, when reason has been abandoned.

Let me back up a few days. Just past a year after the supposed demise of The Russian, we found ourselves in Barcelona investigating a child trafficking ring. Nothing had been reported, but my AI, which we appropriately named, "Oliver", locked into a particular operation there, and using my gift I'd gotten into the digital back entrance of the entity in question (Note: though the AI I developed listened to my every word, via the app an created for it on my phone, it still did not have my gift for cracking into systems. But once I upgraded it, by moving the whole platform to the alien ship hidden beneath the Arctic ice and its quantum computing power, I expected that might change). Thus, after profiling their financials, the AI raised a red flag. Charities, and specifically organizations like this, look a certain way on paper, and so do the bank accounts of the folks who work there. So, while we didn't know exactly what they were doing, or how, we knew that something was amiss. And with innocents involved, we were compelled to dig deeper.

Of course, when we put out the word, the whole crew wanted to go. By intent, we'd not gathered this many of us into one place, since The Russian was murdered. Pretty much all of the usual crew rolled in, except for Roughneck (with his priors, leaving the country can be complicated). On hand we had myself, Marketing Girl, the Heretic, the Zealot, Cousin Kisha, Nia, Voodoo Priestess and Grimes.

Marketing Girl got us a house in Sitges down the coast a bit from Barcelona. The word "vistas", must have been created for such a place as Sitges. It is a strikingly beautiful place. But we had little time to enjoy the wonders of it. MG and Cousin Kisha picking up pastries for the house, was the one treat in which we partook. On the second floor was an outdoor patio, where we congregated to discuss out plans. Grimes got us started by pouring out drink offerings for the fallen, Money and The Russian.

Nia the mute, who somehow had the ability to speak to the animals, signed that she had a plan. She, herself, had been abducted when she was very young. In fact, rescuing her was one of our first big cases. And burning down the house of the street chemist who largely facilitated her abduction, was the second offense against our eternal nemesis, Entropy (even though it would be years before they connected that incident to the group of online vigilantes who'd hacked their bank accounts to return the money they'd stolen from the residents of an assisted living facility in Atlanta). Nia signed, "I think I should infiltrate their operations."

We all groaned, and Cousin Kisha erupted with a hard, "No, that's not happening!"

Nia signed back, "Look, I understand your concern and all, but I'm not that helpless little girl I was way back when." She was right about that. Nia could open her mouth and every creature high and low for blocks would hurry to her call and heed her every command.

She went on, "It's like you always say Blerd, measure twice, cut once. Yes, we know they're dirty. But we don't have the full scope of their operation yet. And without that, it's unlikely that we'll catch everyone involved."

We all nodded in agreement with Nia's argument. So, she went on, "Just give me a week on the inside. If they try to sell me before the week is over, either your AI or our surveillance team will pick it up and the cavalry will come in." This young girl had grown into a powerful woman right before our eyes. And protecting children was her sole passion. Thus, she was determined to be the point of the spear on this particular operation.

Then, just as we were about to wrap up, we heard a commotion downstairs. We all stood up, and as a couple of us moved towards the stairwell, we heard a familiar voice rising up, "What up, y'all?"

"Roughneck?" I replied back.

"You know it…!"

Everyone erupted as the street general, former banger, stepped onto the second-floor patio.

Kisha asked, "How?"

Grimes followed, "Yeah, man, I thought you were on virtual lock down?"

Roughneck grinned slightly, "Well, technically I am. But nawl, shorty you know if we taking down grimy Mofos hurting kids, I had to get me a taste. I know a rapper who was in the game, back when, and I still do security for him every now and then. When I told him what was up, he offered to fly me over in his private jet. No customs, security or anything."

"That's alright, Roughneck." I replied.

"Yeah, when we were kids, neither one of us thought we'd every make it this far."

Then it was time to get down to business.

After buying clothes from one of the kids living on the street in a different part of town (we also gave the teen new clothes along with the payment), we dropped Nia off at the nearest metro rail station. From there she rode Barcelona's mass transit system down to the stop nearest the supposed orphanage. Our surveillance team was already in place. We split the team into two squads of four. Day one in the forward position, we had the Heretic, Kisha, Grimes and Marketing Girl, with them working in pairs of four-hour shifts, two doing surveillance, while the other two chilled in coffee shop down below. The Heretic and Marketing Girl took the first shift, with Kisha and Grimes taking the second shift, from there they rotated every four hours. Squad two, consisting of Zealot, Voodoo Priestess, Roughneck and me were posted up in a hotel room we'd rented five blocks away. We did it this way, because we didn't want to blow our cover by too many Americans so close to the target. Plus, whoever was back at the hotel was expected to continue digging for useful information regarding our target. We had the sense that there were lots of threads yet to be pulled from this sweater. Bottomline, we had eyes on the orphanage twenty-four hours a day.

Day One: Nia sat at the corner of a bank, three blocks away from the orphanage, begging for money. She was run off by bank security three times, but each time she returned to her post. We had some alternative spots in the area, where we could still maintain surveillance, if she was forced to move, but this was our preferred location. At night she slept in the doorway of a side door to the bank. Our night vision tech was of the highest quality, so we had full confidence in our ability to protect Nia.

Day Two: I noticed a man and a woman from the orphanage approach Nia. And though we had the audio, we really didn't need it to understand how the conversation progressed. They approached her and introduced themselves speaking in Spanish. Nia signed back to them, introducing herself. They offered her a hot meal, but Nia played hard to get. Then they mentioned that they planned to have live music that evening for the kids. Nia smiled and signed back, "That would be nice."

At that point, the pair pointed down the street towards their orphanage. So, Nia picked up her cardboard mat, taking care to fold it before tucking it under her arm. Back home, Nia spent at least one weekend a month living on the streets with the street kids. They knew her well, and she did all she could to help them. These missions of ours, gave her a chance to focus on something else beyond the seemingly unending calamity of homelessness in America. Although, this was not America, we were in fact, arguably knee deep into the darkest pillar of our homeless *problem*, human trafficking; and this problem exists in every corner of the globe.

From our rooftop location, I sent a message to the rest of the team, that stated, "Insertion complete. Proceeding to stage two."

Voodoo Priestess looked over at me, "So, that basically means that we're still here on this roof until our shift ends, huh?"

I gave her a look which apparently said everything I was thinking. But Nia going inside did mean that there was no need to keep staring into our scopes twenty-four seven. The next step was to bring the tiny wireless microphones Nia had online. She had to be careful not blow her cover, but after about an hour, we heard the comforting noise of one of the mics coming online. The first mic was to be located wherever she would be sleeping. Since Nia was mute, she tapped on the mic a couple times to alert us that it was operative and in place. She was on the second floor (all of the kids were housed on the second floor and above) Subsequently, we turned up the sound on our end and heard the sweet voices of children approaching Nia, asking her all the questions that children do, when they encounter someone new, someone different.

Day Five: The first couple of days of surveillance, confirmed that this orphanage actually facilitated some legitimate adoptions. Grimes and I vetted each adult who strolled through the front door that didn't work for the orphanage. We confirmed each would-be parent, as well as each staff person that worked for the orphanage. They all checked out. Nia used the color of her scarf on any given day, to communicate the status of things on the inside. All was good.

However, on the fifth night things took a turn. Around two in the morning, three black SUVs pulled up in front of the orphanage. The Heretic and Cousin Kisha were on the roof, while Grimes and Marketing Girl (our team translator and logistics lead) chilled in the suite down below. The rest of us were in a hotel nearly four blocks away, sleeping. The phone sitting on the coffee table right in front of the couch I was sleeping on suddenly chirping loudly. Being a very light sleeper, I sprung up with a quickness to answer it. It was Cousin Kisha, on the line, "Hey, Cuz, we got activity down here. Three large black vans just pulled up. I take them for a government personal protection unit. Which means that the package they're protecting is…"

"Yeah, I know. But it doesn't change anything does it?"

"You right Cuz. A lot of folks want us dead already, what's one more? We're heading down."

I yelled loud enough to wake everyone in the hotel room. "Time to Rock and roll, y'all !!!" Then I said to Kisha, "Switching to my headset. We'll be there in less than five."

Back at the forward position, Kisha roused Roughneck and Marketing Girl, after asking the Heretic to remain on the roof to provide cover from up high for the team. Kisha and Roughneck strode off briskly towards the orphanage, even as we listened in to the mic affixed to Nia's cot. Marketing Girl, with her headset strapped on provided play by play translations to everyone, of any meaningful conversation near Nia, given that not the whole team was fluent in Spanish.

Over our headsets Marketing Girl announced, "They've pulled three of the girls from their beds. One of them is Nia. Move it y'all!"

After the state official's security team had secured the location, two of them came back out to escort the dignitary into the facility.

The Heretic called, "Oh my goodness, y'all won't believe who just stepped out of the middle van. Damn…"

I called out over my headset, "Try to hang back until the rest of us get there. But don't let them take Nia."

"You ain't gotta worry about that…" the brawler replied back. "What's your ETA?" he added.

"Two minutes!" I answered as the four us from the other hotel ran towards the orphanage.

Then I heard it. We all heard it. My heart sank as I heard the head of state call out Nia's undercover name.

Cousin Kisha announced, "Cuz, can't wait. Roughneck rock with me. Heretic, shoot anybody creeping on our six."

"I got you." Replied the Heretic to his fellow veteran from the rafters down a block and across the street.

Kisha approached the outermost security team member and attempted to speak to him in broken Spanish, "Habla usted espanol o Ingles?"

"Yes.", the black suited man replied tersely. "And keep back please, this is official business."

"Sir, are you aware that there is ongoing child trafficking from this establishment?"

At her words, two other heads beyond the one which had intercepted Kisha turned slightly in her direction. Half a beat later, after obviously getting some sort of instruction over their coms, all three men moved quickly towards Kisha in an attempt to apprehend her. But in that moment, Roughneck, who was presenting as a homeless man for this mission, bull rushed the three men, knocking all of them to the ground, except Kisha. As the street fighter got to his feet, he hollered out loud, "Go Kisha!!!"

Kisha then moved quickly towards and beneath the awning which covered the entrance, only to encounter two other men dressed in black with their guns out. As Kisha reached to pull the gun tucked in her back, and the Heretic called out, "Damnit, I don't have a shot..." a scarf wearing blonde woman approaching the entrance from the other direction, smoothly pulled out a pistol from her purse and shot both men in the back of the head before she reached the awning.

Kisha looked at the woman and realized immediately who she was even before she spoke. The blonde speaking in her Russian accent nodded and declared, "I got you sister."

The Heretic cried out, "Oh, my God, I just saw a ghost! I could tell by how she held her strap!"

But as Kisha and the blonde shooter spotted up on either side of the double door entrance to the lobby, a hail of bullets from an automatic burst through the glass tops of the doors.

As this was happening the Heretic, knowing that their opponents were outfitted with body armor, shot two of the men tangling with Roughneck in the leg, which took most of the fight out of them, and allowed Roughneck to disarm them and dispose of the third man quickly.

This was the situation when the Zealot, Voodoo Priestess, Grimes and I arrived. The ladies were pinned down on either side of the door. It was the most chaotic scene I'd ever witnessed in my life, magnified by Nia being on the wrong side of it all.

Voodoo Priestess announced, "I can get to Nia!"

Grimes then seeing that there was another woman flanking the other side of the entrance from Kisha, uttered, "What the…? Who is that?"

I injected, "But can you get out with her? What if there are a couple of these guys guarding her, what then?"

"I'll figure it out; I always do." Voodoo Priestess answered, in a low determined voice.

"Hold up y'all; that looks like…" a zombified Grimes offered, without the will to complete his assertion.

As the Heretic repelled from his perch on the building across the street to the sidewalk, he stated "In a minute they're going to realize that their best option is to bum rush us and make a break for their armored vehicles."

"No doubt!" Roughneck answered.

"Zealot, do you have those flash bombs on you?" The Heretic asked.

"Yeah, I was thinking the same thing." The Zealot answered

The Heretic added, "Voodoo, when this goes down, we'll have their full attention. That's when you snatch Nia from them!" The Heretic and Zealot were our two tactical leads, who were charged with leading us when the need arose.

Grimes stumbled towards the doorway even as the two shooters intermittently fired off bursts of automatic gunfire. Grimes whispered, "Russian…?"

The Zealot asked, "Kisha, how many shooters have automatics behind the door?"

"Just two, but they have an arsenal in the trucks. Grenade launchers and such." The unrivaled intuit replied.

The mystery woman, briefly locked eyes with Grimes, and offered a quick smile, as she took a step back from her position, as did Kisha.

The Zealot said over our coms, "On three, turn your heads, cover your ears and shut your eyes!" On one, he tossed the flash bomb, and we all closed our eyes on three. Boom, went his charges. Then the Zealot, trusting that his plan had worked in the dark of night, moved without hesitation left to right across the entrance from the middle of the street, firing off two shots. Both kill shots found their targets. The Zealot called out, "Clear!", confirming that he'd taken out the automatics.

Kisha and the blonde rolled through the door, mindful to keep low. They immediately began to take fire from two more security team members from their protected positions.

Mumbling and in tears Grimes with his shotgun lowered stumbled towards the entrance, as the Heretic and Zealot strode past him, with obvious purpose in their eyes.

Seeing him, Roughneck grabbed Grimes by the shoulders and dragged him back, "Can somebody come and get this fool?"

But before I could make a move, the one who can move without moving, reappeared at my side with Nia in hand. Reflexively, I embraced the muted Nia, like the daughter she was to me, and to all of us. I was so happy to have her back. Now, we just needed to get out of this alive.

Voodoo Priestess, whispered, "Is that…"

"Yes."

"Thought so, I mean I had an inkling when I did her reading."

"Do you mind getting…"

"Sure, I got it." With a nod she disappeared and reappeared standing next to Roughneck who had Grimes in an old school wrestling hold with his arms wrapped around Grimes' shoulders and his hands locked behind Grimes' head. "Give him to me."

"He's yours, spooky woman." Voodoo Priestess freaked Roughneck out, but he respected the hell out of her. She nodded and then disappeared with Grimes in tow.

A moment later, she reappeared standing next to me and Nia. "You good?" I asked Voodoo Priestess, because I knew that all of that blinking in and out takes a lot out of her.

"I'm fine. No time for nothing else right now."

The Zealot called out, "They're on the move." Referencing the two remaining guards in the lobby.

Quickly my thoughts turned. If we have Nia there was no reason for these fools to fight their way out to their vans. "Nia, this place has a backdoor, right?" She nodded in confirmation.

"I think the package they're protecting has gone out the back door!" Actually, with my gift, I knew that he had.

As Roughneck, Voodoo Priestess, Nia and I rushed around to the rear of the structure, the rest of our team stormed through the lobby. We all arrived in the back ally just in time to see a fourth black van speeding way. These guys were pros, so they'd always had an alternate exit should anything go wrong. Had we'd known the buyer was a head of state, we would have had the rear exit covered. Or more likely, we would have come up with a totally different approach. The Zealot raised his rifle as if to take one final shot at the black van, but I pushed his barrel down. "Bruh, no need for that now."

We all walked back into the orphanage to see most of the staff exiting the storage closet off the lobby. The staff identified the husband and wife team who ran the place. For such a big client, they'd both chosen to work the graveyard shift.

Once we had them seated in the lobby, I asked in English, "What the hell?"

The husband started off with a bunch of threats.

I responded, "Look around this room. What makes you think that you can intimidate us?"

Then he began to spout out a series of lies, when his wife interrupted, "Miguel, stop. Just stop!" The dark-haired woman took a beat, then began telling us about the whole layout and what they were about. In closing she argued, "You've obviously done your homework on us, and you know that there's no way that we, without generous donors could run an orphanage in this part of town. I'm guessing that's what first caught your eye."

"It was one thing." I replied.

"But what you don't understand, is that we never intended to come to this place, we never intended to become this. A year after we opened, we were filled to capacity, but the funding we thought we'd get when we shared our vision for this mission with potential sponsors about the need, and how we could address it, never materialized. Soon after, a local older wealthy man approached us about adopting one of the kids, even though he didn't match our adoptee profile. But he offered to pay us an amount that would cover our rent and operational costs for eight months. So, we took the money and he kept the child. Then about a year later, while we were still struggling, the wife of the man who'd made the large contribution, introduced us to a wealthy couple who were looking to adopt, but didn't want to go through the normal channels that the state requires. They offered to cover our expenses for the year. Then apparently word got out that we were people who could be trusted in such matters. We reasoned, that it was better to sacrifice one or two kids a year, if we could use that money to provide homes, clothing and food for thirty others, who'd be living on the street otherwise and all that comes with that. We chose to believe that these out of scope adoptive parents were benevolent, and trustworthy. We could protect them here. But…" and the woman paused to look at her husband before proceeding. He nodded and she went on, "We were equally sure that more than a few of the donors had bad intent. And still we rationalized it all."

Finally accepting the truth of things, the husband cried out, "We're monsters!!!" before cradling his face in his hands as he sobbed bitterly.

His wife massaged the back of her husband's head as she asked, "What now?"

"What now?" is what I asked myself just as the local SWAT team rushed in.

For better or worse, the couple fessed up regarding everything to the police. Once they mentioned who the buyer was, the Sargent froze for a moment, then made a call to the police chief. During his call, one of the detectives continued to question us there in the lobby. I told him that the "buyer" was in the process of kidnapping our friend, and that they fired upon us when we tried to stop them. Those were the facts.

The detective offered the obligatory, "Well, you should have called us."

"But they'd been gone with the girl by the time you got here."

"Yes, but we could have stopped them before they left the country."

"But could you have, really? I mean given who it was?"

"Perhaps, but as it stands, you and all of you who were armed, are facing gun and discharge charges here in Spain. This is not America. Here you're looking at some serious time. Was it worth it?"

I looked at Nia, "Yes."

The detective nodded in concession.

As the he turned from me to question the others, my thoughts drifted. Seeing this couple huddled together I began to question my understanding of evil. Until that moment, I saw evil as being a state of being where the actor relishes in the cruel actions, internalizing the evil within. But it was clear that these two, still had some semblance of a conscious, even if it had been deeply suppressed for years, like the Germans who worked in the concentration camps for a fool's quest. Sure, some, like psychopaths, are born that way, but most who find themselves in these spaces, never sought it, nor knowingly leapt into it. No, rather they descended into hell one step at a time, like a frog in a pot that slowly comes to a boil. But in that moment, both were contrite and seemingly even relieved that they'd been caught. They were more than ready to spend the rest of their lives behind bars. But I already knew that it would never come to that, because they'd both be dead within a year.

The Sargent was on the phone with those to whom he answered for over an hour, raising his voice often. He was not pleased at all when he returned to the collections of chairs and benches that filled the middle of the lobby.

The Sargent cleared his throat before speaking, "Hmm, since the child was not indeed taken, there will be no prosecution of the *buyer*."

The Detective inquired, "And what about all of these dead bodies?"

The Sargent replied, "They're all foreign nationals, and their government has decided not to press for an arrest. They just want their bodies back. Our government has no taste for this either, since no Spanish citizens were harmed tonight." After sighing, he continued, "But this place is shut down. We have a van coming to relocate the children."

The husband said aloud, "And what about us? Aren't you going to take us with you?"

"No." the Sargent said, and left it there.

The husband looked at the Sargent, while his wife bowed her head accepting what she knew would come. She knew that now since they could no longer serve the needs of their wealthy clients, they'd become a liability on their balance sheets. She'd always known that this was a possibility, though her husband was still, even then, oblivious to it all. The powerful would clean up this mess, as they so often did, quietly, in due time.

We too were on their list of items to be cleaned up, but by sunrise, we let the head of state's people know that we had footage of him visiting the orphanage, and audio recordings of what he said while there. And if something were to happen to us, where we didn't reset the scheduled release of what we had, because say we were imprisoned or dead, an email with what we captured attached, would go out to all of the major media outlets worldwide.

As we headed for the front exit we literally ran into Grimes, who'd final returned from wherever Voodoo Priestess had taken him. Pushing through the rest of us, he embraced The Russian, "Girl, I thought you were dead! We saw the lab results. How...?"

The Russian hushed the stunned Grimes into silence, "Shss..., just accept that I am here with you now. That's all you need to know." Their relationship had always been one free of questions, and in this regard, for The Russian, nothing had changed.

I knew the truth, that The Russian did indeed die, and yet she lives through her remaining two twin sisters. It was clear to me that they lived a common life, interchanging roles with one another seamlessly. If one of them had a partner, they all had a partner. If one had a spouse, they all had a spouse. If one had a child, they all had a child. They shared each other's laughter and tears. They shared each truth, each lie and everything in between.

Beyond me, Voodoo Priestess knew at the very least, some version of the truth. And the way Kisha's gift works, she knew without doubt that The Russian was presenting a façade regarding her life, even if her love for the team, was as true as any love could be.

As we strode away, Marketing Girl simply asked The Russian, "How did you know that we were here?"

The Russian smiled, "I had to lay low for a while, but I was never far away. I came to the belief that you would be here and could use my help." Which meant that even from the grave, per se, she was still tracking our chatter because she knew our online aliases, and our coded vernacular.

As we all readied to depart, with each of us going our own way (as a safety precaution), Roughneck gave Cousin Kisha a quick hug, "Y'all go on. I've got to put in some work while I'm here."

Kisha gave her sometime paramour a quizzical look.

"Well, old boy who flew me out here, needs me to provide security for a party he's attending up the coast a bit. That was the deal, for me hitching a ride here. Hey, some of us have to work for our dinner."

Mid-morning the next day, as Grimes and I boarded a train headed east to our departure sites (he would be flying out Paris, and I Amsterdam, the following day). Grimes continued his coded debriefing regarding The Russian, "I know that I'm a different kind of cat, so I guess she's the kind of woman I need, you know. A different kind of girl."

And though I was in a different rail car, and he could not see me, I nodded in silent agreement, knowing that he'd never know just how different she and her sisters were.

Aqualung

My phone rang, glancing at the clock I saw that it was six in the morning, a Saturday morning in fact. "You sleep?" the voice over the line inquired.

"I ain't now, that's for sure. What's up, Grimes?"

"Do you remember that thing I told you about that might or might not be true, but I kind of thought that it was, mostly?"

"Grimes," I started in frustration and then modulated my voice a bit, "you've told me quite a few things that fit that bill."

"Hmm, I guess so. But I'm talking about the one that involves the kid at the lake."

"yeah…"

"Well, there's some chatter online about of bunch Area 51 alien conspiracy bros arranging a meetup at the lake just outside of Saint Paul's tomorrow morning to investigate the matter. They may not have pitchforks, but I'm sure that they all have camera phones, which might be worse."

I wasn't too sure about his word choice in the moment, but I didn't want this oh so early conversation to get sidetracked over semantics. "Yeah, I hear you. So, what do you want to do?"

"You already know. Who can we get to roll with us on a day's notice?"

"Hmm, Roughneck is never busy, but otherwise, I'll need to put the word out and see who's available."

By that evening, I was walking the concourses of Minneapolis – Saint Paul International Airport, in the land of ten thousand lakes. I grabbed my bag and posted up in baggage claim to wait for my compadres to land. One by one they arrived, Nia the mute animal whisperer, who is also a veterinarian, missed homecoming at Tuskegee University to join us. I took the opportunity to lean in and ask, "Are you okay with this?"

Nia, who'd grown into the most beautiful young woman, with the most perfect dark complexion, signed back to me, "I'm fine. In fact, this is the kind of assignment which speaks to my heart." When we first encountered Nia, she'd been taken by a child trafficking ring. We rescued her, and ever since, she's had a heart for the wellbeing of children and young adults. In her mind, she had to be here. Protecting the innocent was her life's work, her reason for being.

The next to arrive was Roughneck. He gave me a quick look, as he marched into baggage claim toting a cold one, he'd bought right after deboarding his flight. I knew right away, that his flight had been turbulent and he needed a moment to settle and drink his beer. Or as he would say, he *needed to get situated*. But I knew he'd be okay and ready to go afterwards.

The last to arrive was Grimes, lord of the digital underworld. "Sorry, I'm late. I missed my flight, and had to fly standby on the next one. Y'all know how ATL traffic can be." In this instance, we all understood and knew that this was bullshit. Grimes had a legitimately traumatizing experience in the airport some years before, right after Money was murdered. He'd not flown domestically since then, until this mission. He flew up because even he had to concede that an overnight drive from Atlanta to Saint-Paul was unrealistic. But we didn't sweat him on the matter.

Once all four of us were loaded up and rolling down the street, I asked Grimes to give us the latest. He obliged, "Yeah, so the meet up spot posted online for these *investigators*, is the state park visitor center. The irony of that, were this kid actually an alien, huh? Anyway, the way I see it, we can either mingle with the crowd and work to control things from the inside. You know like pushing them away from where the kid actually is. Or we can go find the kid for ourselves and skirt him out of here. I mean we have better intel than the mob does, so I'm thinking that we have a very good shot at finding him first."

I replied "Hmm, I like the way the way you're thinking, but maybe we can do both. One of us can meet up with the mob, and try to mislead them, or at the very least keep the rest of us informed as to their whereabouts. While the rest of us find the kid. Do you feel like outing one of your online aliases today? You know, drop a hint or two that you might be so and so. I'm sure they'll hang on your every word?"

"Yeah, but all my digital masks, have value, and I just burned one last year. Do you know how long it takes to build them up? I don't want to become totally useless in these digital backstreets."

"That's fair."

"But in the end, you know that I'd do anything for the kid, even if that means becoming the shiny object in the crowd's peripheral vision." I knew well that Grimes is gifted at playing things up and soaking up attention, especially with the likes of those in attendance that day.

"I know, Grimes. Nia, Roughneck and I will find the kid and get him out of the area. While you roll with the crowd."

After dropping Grimes off down the street from the visitor center, I took my crew back up into the woods. I pulled out a map of the state park, and pointed to a spot on it. "This is where we're going," I announced. By this point, I'd come into full awareness that I did indeed have a unique gift, in that pretty much anything I looked for, I'd find. I wasn't sure how it worked underneath, but I knew well how to leverage it. In an instance like this, if I saw a map, I'd know right away, if what I was looking for was within the span of that map, and if it was, where on the map said item was. Growing up, I'd always score within the ninety-ninth percentile when taking multiple choice tests. I just always knew the right answer, when I saw it.

Having driven our rental car as far as I dared through the previous night's freshly fallen snow, I pulled over and announced, "We walk from here."

Always ready Roughneck snapped back, "Let's do it!" Dude was born ready, but these days, he used his gifts for good. Nia followed behind the two of us, as I led the way. We had a decent walk ahead of us to the point on the map I'd identified.

On the far side of the lake, Grimes was mic'd up, so that we could hear the chatter around him in our ear pieces. Over the airwaves, we heard the random pronouncements, "Dude, I'm so pumped!" And, "Aliens, dude, mother freakin' aliens!!!" I imagined most of them holding up their phones and capturing the crowd around them.

As we neared our destination, a far-off secluded corner of the lake, one of its many "fingers", a murky patch of water full of dead reeds still standing in winter's morning light, I caught sight of what appeared to be a humanoid image floating above the shimmering waters. I thought perhaps it was a passing refraction of light, playing a proverbial trick on me. But it persisted.

I called to Roughneck, "You see that?"

"Looks like a mirage, don't it?"

"Yeah…" I waited a second and then called out, "Hello?"

Then I heard a murmur coming back across the waters, it sounded like "Burred", but then it called a second time, "Blerd…" In that moment, my mind, if not my consciousness was transferred back to the eighteen seventies, when I'd last heard this same voice, in the body of another.

As he neared the shore hovering just in front and above us, I could see indeed, that it was the Engineer, the time traveler who had sought to change history, before he was snatched away by the Time Lords (see *Clocks* in "Soo… Volume One"). I too had sought to stop him, for at least in this current version of reality Black people survived. I've always been one who believed that as long as there's life, there's hope. The Engineer did not agree.

"How?" I asked. The Time Lords are very strict and they watch the timeline very carefully, for those who breach the rules set forth by the universe.

"Oh, I'm not really here. This is just my projection from the future. See, after serving my time here, I made it my life's mission to learn everything I could about how the Time Lords manage to see all. In the process of doing that, I found a loophole in their policing scheme. They have the ability to check for many things, but they cannot track energy passing back and forth across time. It's a quantum thing. Eventually, I learned how to project an image of myself back in time. And since this image is wholly energy, they won't be able to detect what I'm doing until it's too late. But what I lack in physical form, I more than make up for in light and sound." He lifted his hand towards one of the fir trees behind us, and with a low rumble, a beam of sound ruffled the needles on the tree so, that most of the fresh snow on it fell to the ground.

Nia signed to me, "How did he know that we would be here?"

As he floated towards the three of us, he asked, "What, that a mob of young men would be here today looking for a dolphin boy? I googled it."

"Damn." I whispered.

The Engineer laughed, "Dude, if you hadn't interfered, we wouldn't still be dealing with this foolishness."

"…and most likely, I wouldn't exist either."

"Well, everything has a cost, don't it?"

"Guess so, that's why you did time."

"Touché. Nonetheless, I'm here for the child. And your being here, tells me that the boy's habitat is in this part of the lake, which is good. Because though I can't funnel enough energy through time to heat this entire lake, I can make this little inlet boiling hot, hot enough to force the child out of the water."

I couldn't help but ask, "Why?"

"Sorry bro, that was my mistake the last time we tussled, telling you all my business. Not gonna happen. But my research suggests that if the mob should find this boy's body, it will increase the likelihood of setting off a chain of events that will at last force an accountability and positively impact the lives of many people of color across the world. Thus, I suggest y'all move, lest you want to get fried or shook."

"Likelihood?"

"Dude, even with quantum computing, we're still reduced to probabilities when it comes to changing history. The mob finding this boy, and the government being exposed, moves the meter a good two to three percent."

"Dude?" I sighed. In truth, the Engineer was an anarchist. He'd vocally disagree, but his actions showed otherwise. Basically, he's decided that the future cannot be any worse than the current model, so he's willing to burn it all down, assuming that what replaces it to be better for black folks. And regardless of what the odds were, my complaint against him remained the same as it did over a century ago, when we first met. What gives him the right to arbitrarily of his own accord do this thing, even if a child's life weren't in question?

Roughneck stepped forward, "Dude, I've never met you before, but you really appear to be the asshole, everyone told me you were. Nonetheless, we're talking about a child. Even assholes know enough not to hurt children."

"Look Roughneck, and yes, I do my homework, I'm here to save our race, and if a failed government science experiment has to be sacrificed to save my people, so be it. I know you're a down for the cause brother, and you're known for doing what needs to be done. But being hooked up with this kumbaya brother, is not a good look for you. And if you want to remain in the game and the change to come, back the hell up. I need to get on with this before those new age frat boys decide to come this way."

With that, the image of The Engineer was replaced with that of a portal hovering above our section of the lake. Nia responded by rushing to the water's edge and thrusting her hands in the water. Without a word, I knew what she was doing, she was telling all of the wildlife she could to leave the area.

At the same time, I called out to Roughneck, "Quick. I don't think he can see or hear us while he's doing this. And that fool still told me something I think we can use."

"Damn, Blerd." Roughneck offered.

As energy began flowing from the portal and heating the lake, I removed my laptop from my backpack and I explained myself to Roughneck, "Well, he confirmed that he can only send a limited amount of energy back through time, otherwise he would have simply boiled the entire lake. Then the news reports will simply mark this as another mass fish die off or something, and the Time Lords will be none the wiser. So, we can assume that he's boiling as much water as he can afford, like one would cast the largest net you could to catch a particular fish."

"So…?" Roughneck asked.

"So, we don't need to stop him completely. All we need to do, is to diminish his ability enough to thwart his plans."

"Thwart?"

"You know what I mean. Hey, call Grimes and tell him, to tell the mob, that the alien will appear above the water over this way and that they should all begin videoing over this way now."

Nia returned to us, as Roughneck was calling Grimes and I was connecting to the cellular towers covering the area. I explained as I continued on, "He's gonna want to broadcast his micro wave energy into the water. We just need to identify what wavelength we need to broadcast at to counter it. Hopefully, I can use the cellular network up here to do that, or at least to cancel out as much of it as I can."

Roughneck asked, "But we're too far away for any audio from their cell phones to reach here, aren't we?"

"Yes, you're correct. But we're not using their audio feed, but the network itself. And the more phones that are engaged the more microwave activity that will pass through the local towers."

As the water below me began to stir, over my earpiece, I could hear the rowdy mob noticing the refraction in the sky above our side the lake. And as the Engineer was sending more and more energy into the lake, the brighter the anomaly in the sky appeared to the mob. But the more they used their cell phones to record the hole in the sky floating above the western shore, the more active the cell phone tower above us. Having hacked the cell tower's network, I was able to tweak its outbound microwave signal to my liking.

Then, as I was focused doing my thing with my laptop, out of the corner of my eye I saw Nia moving towards the water about fifty yards from me, then she broke into a run, before diving head first into the lake. I stood up immediately and raced with Roughneck towards the point where she dived in. We reached the water's edge just as Nia surfaced with a young man in tow. His skin was so pale that it appeared to be translucent. Roughneck and I stepped into the water, each of us grabbing an arm of the waterlogged teen, carrying him to shore. Beyond the reeds the boy convulsed as Roughneck flipped a picnic table over as some sort of shield behind which we could hide, as the floating image of the Engineer took form once more and descended towards us. We knew that we needed to move, and with a quickness.

But then the strangest thing happened. A fog as thick as pea soup descended upon us. So thick was this fog that one could not see one's own fingertips on an extended arm.

Roughneck stuck his head up and exclaimed, "What the…"

I tugged on Roughneck's arm pulling him back down behind the table, as energy beams illuminated the fog to our left and right. I knew that the further we moved away from the beach the less likely one of these pot shots from the Engineer would to strike us, but the boy literally had a death grip on the bench, refusing to move. My first priority was to secure the boy.

There we huddled, protecting the child, for what seemed an eternity. That is, until we heard something other than the sound of high-pitched energy beams exciting the cold air. At first, it sounded like a low buzz, but as the sound grew louder, I could hear the distinct sound of human voices. It was the online mob. Some of them had sprinted over to our corner of the lake while others continued videotaping.

Roughneck tugged on my arm, as to make a dash for the tree line. But before we could rise up, I heard a voice from above, "Oh, oh…" It was the lamenting voice of the Engineer. And with that he disappeared.

It was only then, that I pivoted from protecting the boy's life, and back to saving him from the mob. In that moment, I handed Roughneck the car keys and motioned for him to get the boy out of there. I stood up and walked towards the sounds of the mob. It was then, that I heard the distinct sound of Grimes' voice among the crowd. I called out, "Dude!" not wanting to use Grimes' online name or his real name around the masses.

Hearing my voice, Grimes called me by my real name. Then through the fog, I saw him. "Dude…", I said again. Then lowering my voice, I said to him, "Y'all were right on time."

"Man, I heard over our com; was that really the Engineer?"

"Yeah, it was or at least his image that he projected from the future. I'm sure that having a crowd of fanboys documenting and uploading his appearance in the twentieth century, would be an event that would be noticed by the Time Lords."

"Nobody likes this guy, huh?"

A moment later, as the fog began to lift, Nia appeared to my left coming from the beach. She signed to Grimes and me, "What happened?"

"You tell us." I said back to her, as I reached out to give her shivering frame a hug.

She signed back, "Well, the first part was standard procedure for me. I could sense that the fish in the water were aware of his presence, and from that I knew exactly where he was.

"And the fog?" I asked.

"Yeah, that… In the moment, when I saw that the Engineer was intent on killing boy, something within me shifted, and a new awareness came upon me. It was like I became one with the mist, like it was just another appendage, that I controlled like an arm or a leg."

"Well, it worked. He couldn't see his target and was just firing randomly."

"What about the boy?" Nia signed.

"Roughneck got him out of here. I'm sure that none of the overzealous would-be online influencers, will try Roughneck in real life, if they do happen to bump into them in the woods. In that sense, it's a wrap. But unfortunately, we're going to need to relocate the boy somewhere far away from here."

"So, what is he?" Grimes queried.

"I don't know, not in full. But I tell you this, he's not any of the things they say online. Before we arrived, I did some digging, and I found a couple of things. First, his mother was a champion free form diver, who could hold her breath for up to fifteen minutes per dive. Secondly, the research group that was involved in this matter was known for testing the effects of RNA across generations. If I had to guess, they found that the boy was even more gifted than his mother. I wouldn't be surprised, if he only has to come up for air every thirty minutes or so."

Nia signed, "So, how did he wind up here?"

"I don't know. But he may have some sort mental deficiency, which may have gotten him kicked out of whatever research project that he was a part of. Then again, being basically a lab rat to the researchers, they may not have invested in fulfilling his needs as a child, since they might not have had any intention on him being anything more. But I really don't know, and I'm not real sure that he'll ever be able to tell us, and I'm sensing that someone has been taking care of him on the low. But one thing I can say with certainty, is if you two do the research and find a place for him, I'll do everything in my power to make it happen."

Grimes nodded, "Yep, we got you." Then he added, "And the Engineer?

"He's not going to quit." I answered. "So, like it or not, we're going to need to deal with him. Once we get the boy squared away, we'll need to convene everyone to figure out just how you combat a man from the future, a man who knows what's coming?"

Nia and Grimes, bowed their heads, as each acknowledged the difficulty of the challenge. Nia signed simply, "Damn…"

The Girl (Part 3) – The Hereafter

Well, the Girl finally got your boy. So, here I am writing you from The Hereafter. Oh, don't weep for me. I knew it couldn't last. I knew early on that if I stayed with her, it would not end well for me.

Of course, there were clues all along the way, like when she told me, "The guy I talk to twice a month says that I'm a sociopath, but that I could be a psychopath. Psychopath sounds a lot sexier, doesn't it?"

That's my Girl, always striving for the next level.

Well, the day that everything went down started like any other. As I waited for the school bus (I must be the only senior in the entire nation without a car), some assholes drove damn near up on the curb through a puddle, drenching me and the others where we stood, even as we tried to escape. The guy in the passenger side window, laughed and gave us the bird, as they drove off. I didn't tell the others that I knew those guys, lest they turn on me, since I was likely the real target of their morning bullying. I was sure that they'd strike again once I got to school. Bullies enjoy victory laps, lots of them. So, I fully expected them to celebrate this "win," with even more bullying once I got to school. I so wanted to be anywhere, but where I was in that moment. Thus, was the paradox called my life. I enjoyed school, but absolutely hated most of the people in it. Anyway, some good Samaritan stopped and loaded everyone at our stop into her van, except me. She leaned forward enough to look at me as she said, "Hey, you can find your own way, right?" Once again, the Universe teased some sort of relief, only to pull the ball away again. Though, from my mother's perspective, she believed that bullies are simply a fact of life, that I'd simply have to learn how to overcome. But she was more upset that the "good Samaritan" opted to leave me behind. She'd say, "If your skin was a little lighter, and your hair a little straighter, I bet she'd have picked you up!"

But me being me, I simply nodded softly to assuage the Samaritan's guilt for leaving me, the soaking wet teenage black boy, behind. The bus was mad late, so I decided that I needed hike to school. With any luck, I'd get there before second period started. But I think we've established by now, that luck held a grudge against me, before I was even born. In fact, at times it seemed that luck held a murderous rage for me, the source of which I knew not.

So then, I heard a car honk behind me, and I jumped just a bit, assuming that it was another privileged asshole looking to harass me. Then I heard the voice call out behind me, "Hey, you…!!!"

I turned to see the Girl. "Yo, Scratchy. Let's play hooky today!" she yelled.

Amazingly, I answered, "I don't know…" as a pain shot up my leg, the leg which she broke when she ran me over a while back. And though it was mostly healed by this point, it still ached when it rained.

"Come on, it'll be fun!"

"Fun for who?" Asked. "The last time I rode off with you, I wound up in the emergency room being treated for burns."

"Hey, I didn't think human flesh was flammable, you know. I mean, people in the circus eat fire all the time. Maybe, it was your cologne?"

"I don't wear cologne. But regardless, I'm graduating in two weeks! And I can't afford any more stints in the hospital, if I want to graduate with my class."

"Walking with your class is overrated. I didn't walk with my class either and look at me. All I had to do was show up for summer school a few days, smile at the assistant principle, and my diploma magically appeared in my mailbox."

"I don't think that will work for me." Plus, I didn't have the social status in our school to smile about anything, without being aggressively asked, "What you smiling 'bout?" Which was typically followed by a less than flattering adjective. (Note: There's nothing "micro" about the aggression in high school, but that's a story for another day)

"Okay, so you're scared. And yes, sometimes things have gone left *a bit* for us, I will admit. But I promise you, I no longer associate with witches, cults or politicians anymore. I've learned my lesson!"

Frankly, I was stunned into silence by her use of the phrase "a bit". In my hesitation, I looked back into her smiling face, saying nothing, hoping that my silence would speak for me.

Then her lips moved. "Look, you're my boy. So, if you like, I'll make sure that you're back on campus before your last period starts. And I brought you a gift." She held out an apple through the rolled down window.

"I don't think that…" In that fraction of a second, lost in her smile, I once again, dislodged myself from reason. "Sure." I took the apple from her hand and climbed into the passenger seat. I'm such a chump.

As we drove towards the expressway, she went on and on about the places we'd visit and all the fun we were going to have, just the two of us hanging out. All of that nonsense lasted until we'd gotten onto the expressway, when she offhandedly mentioned, "Oh, I need to make a stop. Won't take more than five minutes."

I cringed at her words, "I need to make a stop.", for they were most often the precursor to my own wellbeing being threatened. Thusly, I gave her the side eye, but she carried on pronouncing as though she didn't see me. And once again, my powers of invisibility were the only constant in my life.

So, we're driving for a minute, eventually exiting the highway somewhere on the north side of town, which traditionally was the white part of town. I wanted to ask the Girl where she was taking me, then I realized that it didn't really matter. Even if she were taking me to the gates of hell, I wasn't going anywhere. So, as we were driving along in a very nice subdivision, the Girl stopped and backed up about a hundred feet. She jumped out of the car and ran across the street, picking up a brown box from the front porch. Smiling, she returned to the car, and after ripping off the address label and tossing the package in the backseat, she then quickly hopped back into the driver's seat, a la Santa Clause and drove off.

Flabbergasted, I looked at her, "Did you just…?"

"No, it's not what you think." She said before I could even get my question out. "You'll see."

Deeper into the subdivision (though, the word *Estates*, posted on the signage as we drove in, was for once, an accurate description of such a place), we pulled up to a very posh estate. "We're here!" she said in a state of euphoria which seemed unwarranted. I mean I'm from a paycheck to paycheck situation, but I don't look at riches in envy, or something to be aspired to. I see money as a means to security, but the lives of the rich and famous have otherwise, never floated the boat for me, if you get what I mean. But affluence, or even the appearance of affluence was like crack to the Girl. And though we're diametrically opposed in this particular core belief, her blatant materialism was never an issue for me, because "A" she was fine, and "B" she seemed incline to allow me to roll around town with her. So, yes, I was a fool, *but I was her fool*. And at that point in my life, that asinine statement made all the sense in the world to me.

We parked on the street along with several sporty cars, all guests like us I supposed. My jaw dislodged at the sight of all of these souped up rides. But the Girl paid these fly rides all the attention one pays to a single grain of sand on a beach. But of course, I would have been all so happy with any one of them. She nodded towards the package she'd tossed in the rear seat. I got the hint and grabbed the box and head up the driveway behind her.

So, as we strolled past more expensive cars, like the shiny Land Rover, the two-seater Jag, and lastly, the totally tricked out Audi full of every after-market accessory one could imagine, I gasped. Around back past the cars and the basketball hoop (for some a symbol of identity that black folks with money keep either to show others that they're still down, or for others as something of their past that they want to hold on to), was a rear basement door, with an outer security door. As the Girl rang the bell, I noticed that the two rear basement windows were coated in blackout tint, so that no one could see inside.

Shortly, a short dude, about my height, but with a full beard, pulled the inner door open, "Yo, Calvin! Your girl is here." Then he pulled the door open to let us both inside. Calvin turned from his workstation towards us, while notably four members of his crew were sitting on bar stools around a big rectangular table, all with extra-large coffees beside their laptops. It's clear that they are preparing to do something or the other. While three other crewmembers were seated on a large couch playing an online video game against some squad from another part of the world. A girl on the couch called out to the crew sitting at the table, "Hey, we got y'all in the spot, so y'all just need to rake. Feel me...?"

"Ya, ya, ya..." one of the guys laughed as he imitated the great old schooler, Busta Rhymes.

Calvin, offered us a "Just a second..." Then he spun from his own laptop again, to stand before us. I stepped back a bit, as I saw that Calvin was like six-four or something. He gave the Girl a quick hug. "Nice to see you...!"

She replied back, "It's good to see you too."

Calvin asked, "So, what's with the box?"

"Oh, I brought you a gift. My assistant here, Scratchy picked it out. So, I hope it's something nice."

HER ASSISTANT??? What the hell…?

"Oh, cool…" He reached for the box and I gave it to him. He pulled out his keychain, a tiny doohickey, with a number of tools on it, one if which was a small blade. As he opened the box he exclaimed, "Oh, it's one of those robots that vacuums your floor… sweet! With these crummy friends of mine over here all the time, this is perfect!"

Somewhat randomly, or so it seemed at first, one of the guys around the table called out, "I'm past the interior firewall."

Calvin answered, "Good intel, huh?"

"Damn straight!", the dude yelled.

The dude who opened the door, took a seat on the stool by the door, with a copy of some book called "So… Volume 1" I thought to myself, what kind of doofus titles a book "So…"? Anyway, it's clear that he's the *whatever* guy on the team. Meaning that he's the guy opening the door, running out to pick up lunch or *whatever* they ask.

A blonde headed young woman sitting with the guys around the table, offered "Jose, you're right. I'm seeing what looks like account data, but most of the fields are encrypted."

The linebacker looking dude at the end of the table, who'd not said a word or looked up since we entered the basement, answered, "As expected. I'm on it."

In that moment, I realized just what these cats were doing. They were a team of hackers, hacking who knows what?

The Girl asked Calvin, "So, do you have it? What we talked about?"

"Oh, yeah. Here it is." Calvin pulled a credit card from his front pocket. "It has your name on it and everything. But remember, you can only use it in one place! No more, got it?"

"Got it!" she answered with a shit eating smile.

Minutes later after Calvin and the Girl reminisced regarding their time in middle school together, and how it was so odd that they both were in Atlanta now.

So, as soon as we were outside and far enough from the basement door, not to be heard, I spurted, "You know what they were doing back there, right?"

"Playing video games, duh…?"

Must be nice to be so simple, "No, the folks at the tables. They were hacking into bank accounts or something…"

"Look Scratchy, you'll get a lot further in life if you just remember this simple rule, don't ask questions for answers you don't want to hear. I made that mistake with my parents."

"Huh?"

"Dude, forget all that. It's shopping time!"

So, we headed straight to Buckhead and Lenox Square Mall. Along the way, I pondered, why Calvin, who, from where I stood, had every advantage would sully his hands so? He just had to follow the road laid out before him, to inherit the same socioeconomic status as his parents. And yet, there he was in his basement leading a criminal enterprise. It occurred to me that perhaps the worst part of privilege, was the existential blindness which came with it. I mean when you're up twenty-five points in the fourth quarter in this Big Game called life, you run the ball. Everybody knows that, right? Well, maybe not everybody, but you get my point. For most in his position, the risk reward meter, clearly says to go sit your ass down somewhere. But no, not this fool. Anyway…

Pulling into our parking spot at Lenox, I realized that Saks Fifth Avenue never stood a chance. Round and round we went through the glittering aisles. She slayed, while I carried the accumulating bounty. Almost three hours later, I wobbled behind her loaded down with the day's haul. "Wasn't that the most awesome experience, ever?" she asked.

I had no answer. Well, none that seemed wise to say. As I closed the trunk, and walked towards the passenger door, the Girl stood next to the driver's door clearly pondering one of life's great questions. "You know Phipps Plaza, is just right there?"

I knew where she was going, figuratively. "Didn't Calvin say…"

She cut me off, "I know what Calvin said. But if I weren't meant to shop there the universe would have never put it right there across the intersection, right?" It should be noted, that while the Girl's middle-class socioeconomic status was superior to my own domestic situation, her status was not that of the Calvins of the world. However, at all times, she held an ace of Hearts up her sleeve. It wasn't useful in every occasion (like getting equal pay, or having folks pay attention to the words coming from her mouth), but when it came to interpersonal interactions, it was a damn showstopper. She was drop dead gorgeous. But having such power can lead to hubris. This was such moment, I feared.

So, fifteen minutes later, we're at Phipps Plaza (yes, just getting out of the parking lot at Lenox, crossing the street and finding another parking place, can take fifteen or twenty minutes). We Atlantans consider our traffic as a form of purgatory. Regardless of your destination, you've got to do your time behind the wheel, on these burning sands we call streets. Only Prometheus knows our suffering.

As the Girl exited the car, she made a move as though she were leading troops into battle, "Charge…!!!" she called out. It was corny as hell, but she was so basic in that way. I'm not sure that she ever read a book without pictures. Although, it should be said that she excelled at life hacks. If she had a test coming up, she found a way to get a copy of it. If she failed a class, she'd either get the grade changed to passing or at least an incomplete. Hell, she'd nearly gotten my black ass killed on multiple occasions and there I was carrying her bags, in a place that I hated.

"Okay…" I softly answered, as my descent into a raging retail inferno continued its downward spiral.

Mercifully, two hours later, we were ready for our final checkout. Of course, I had no shot by this time to make it back to our side of town for my final class of the day. But I blame myself. I knew better.

So, while the cashier was ringing up the Girl's latest haul, I noticed three white men, each alone, shopping in that same department. They were all dressed nicely (not unexpected in Buckhead), but none of them had pulled anything off the rack, for their hands were all empty. Seeing all of this, my junior black man instincts kicked in, and I moved so that I was in the Girl's line sight. At last catching her eye, I moved my eyes slowly to each of the suited guys stationed all around us.

Well, the Girl froze for a moment, staring down at the items being rung up. Then she began digging through her purse as she said, "Just a minute, I've got to find my card." Pulling things out one by one, the last item she pulled out before Calvin's credit card, was 22 caliber pistol.

The hell…!!! I didn't know the Girl was packing! My heart sank. Not only was my Mama gonna beat my ass for missing class, if I got shot and she had to leave her job to come down to the hospital, she'd to kill me! #Betteroffdead. And there I was, frozen like a deer staring into headlights, really bright ones at that.

However, the cashier ringing her up didn't flinch. Instead she said, "Oh, that's cute honey, but all you're gonna do with that is upset somebody, unless you hit them between the eyes. You need to get yourself something like this." The cashier then proceeded to pull out her 45. "This will stop any fool." Note, one thing about Atlanta, regardless of age, gender or race, anyone can be strapped.

The Girl nodded as she handed over her credit card, "You know, I never thought about that. I'll upgrade as soon as I get a chance." And she actually flashed a smile, though it was a nervous one.

The cashier woman, ran the card once, twice and thrice, but no dice. On the third failure, the suited and booted guys closed in, with one asking, "Ma'am, we're going to need for you to come with us."

"Who? Me? Why? Because my card was declined. Don't you know this is embarrassing enough, without you accosting me?"

"Ma'am, the card you used is a fraudulent card, used by a criminal organization, which has been targeting retailers in the area. We're going to need to ask you a few questions."

The Girl paused for a half a second, and then spurted. "Oh, this isn't my card. It's his!"

She said this as she looked my way, but stupid me, I turn around to see who she's talking about? But not seeing anyone behind me, I finally realized that she meant me.

"Oh no, officer. That's not my card!" I convulsed.

The Girl argued, "He's lying. He gave me the card this morning! I thought he was one of these young rappers or something, you know?"

"Ma'am, it doesn't matter, you're the one that tried to use the card."

They proceeded to put cuffs on both the Girl and me. Then the cashier shook her head at me and asked, "Why aren't you in school?"

I wanted to say, "Damn good question, ma'am. One which I've been thinking about all day." But instead, I just lowered my head and did the walk of shame, as they led us away.

As we rode along in the back of the undercover police car to the station, the Girl leaned over towards me and whispered, "Remember, no snitching…"

At the station, the cops handed me over to a Federal agent, who informed me that what we did was considered wire fraud, which was a federal crime. Honestly, I didn't know quite how to process that, so I sat there stupefied. Just then my mother stepped into the interrogation room. She looked at me like I'd never seen her do before, "Boy!" Then she said to the federal agent, "Say again, what you just said."

He repeated himself and then added, "But your son here, is not being cooperative…."

"Fool…!!! I can't believe that you're this big of a damn fool! If you don't sign them damn papers so that we can get out of here, I'm gonna beat your ass twice! Once for hanging with that heifer, after I told you to leave her ass alone. And again, for being so stupid, not to see that she's playing you. Boy…!!! Got me down here, off my job for some bullshit! Keep on doing this foolish shit, and you'll have us living out a box on Ashby street…". The whole, we're about to be homeless, was my mama's go to move, to end any chastisement of me. Now, as I got older, I learned that much of what my mama said wasn't particularly true, only something to shut me up. But the whole being bitterly close to being homeless, thing was all too true.

As we left the interrogation room on our way to the woman to whom I was to give my statement, we saw the Girl in the hallway, on her way back to her cell after giving her own statement. She smiled and mouthed, "No Snitching…"

So, what did I do? Did I take one for the team? Did I keep my mouth shut?

Oh, hell nah! Who you talking to? I was much too small to go to big boy prison. I sang like a canary that had been drinking all afternoon. Please…

After my virtuoso performance, the feds pulled off this big sting, snagging up Calvin and his whole crew. Turns out they were a part of some much larger crime syndicate. Who knew?

After doing ninety days in Club Fed (which really got my tennis game into proper form) and getting my high school diploma in the mail, the Feds relocated me and mama to Hereafter, Colorado.

Oh wait, y'all didn't think that I was really dead, did you? Well, on paper, I'm pretty much dead. But in reality, me and mama are off doing a new thing, with new identities. Feds even got her a decent job, which she can do from home, which actually pays more than the two to three crummy jobs she worked back in Atlanta, just to keep us off the streets.

And the Girl? Well, once she got of out jail (she snitched too, after first trying to pin it all on me) she developed a modest business online as an "influencer", but like a low level one. So, we're not talking being a YouTube star or anything like that. But more so, an influencer who built a following of dudes who want to see her pose in scanty clothing. And for a modest fee, they can visit her website to see the "Not Safe For Work" stuff. But when you consider some of the other lines of work she aspired to in the past, like being an assassin, a witch in a coven that offered live sacrifices (actually, I was the lamb she offered to join their club) and a party clown, her brilliant idea to meet would-be sugar daddies, which as you might imagine caused more chaos than cash flow, not to mention getting her ass beat by the disapproving wives, a couple of times.

But you know what? I wish her all the best. Yeah, I see clearly now that I was her fool. But two things can be true. To this day I believe that she had a genuine affinity for me, even at times referring to me as her boyfriend. But it's equally true that she was just a despicable human being (regardless of whether she was clinically a sociopath or psychopath). The real question is who was I to allow myself to be in such a *relationship*? That question has followed me all these years. But as my mother would always tell me, "You were young and stupid. It happens. Move on."

Yes, Mama.

Carla and the Whale

First, let me say up front, I'm a fool, a complete and utter fool. My Daddy saw the Crayola on the wall early on with me, and told me so, repeatedly. But he said that it's better to be a fool and know it, than to be one and not know it. But it wasn't until I was grown, that I realized just how right he was, 'cause I kept finding myself in situations. So, here I am. A fool, whose hibernation chamber didn't open until long after it should have. I was to be a worker in building this space colony on this slightly smaller Earth, full of mostly black and brown folks. When I finally did wake up, all I had were the clothes on my back, and whatever was in my locker beneath my pod. And somehow, despite my ability to find myself in situation after situation, I'm still alive. Case in point...

Just like that she was gone. After some amazing sex on the beach (no, it's not just some overpriced drink), she'd gone for a dip in the water just to cool off. But then all of a sudden, some creature from the deep rose up, swallowed Carla whole and then just as quickly returned to the watery abyss with her. Hammer in hand I ran to the point where she disappeared. Then I felt it, or more correctly, didn't feel it. Like the lakes back home, this bad boy just dropped off. But in this regard, it was no different than the watering holes I swam in as a kid, except that it had an appetite for pretty girls.

Instinctively, I reeled back half a step to solid ground, to grab a deep breath, then dove hammer first into the darkness. I allowed my hammer to pull me down, just hoping that this critter hadn't scurried off somewhere else to enjoy its meal. Finally reaching the bottom, I noticed a light in the darkness. Moving closer, I could see that it was the thing that had swallowed Carla. The damn thing had a light between its eyes, like you see in National Geographic or some online videos. As crazy as that was to see, it was even crazier to see a couple of the creature's mini-me's huddled together in some sort of cave it must have burrowed for them.

Then it struck me that this heifer was catching live prey to offer to its kids. I've seen other animals do this kind of thing to teach their kids how to survive. So, when she opened her mouth, I was pleased to see Carla float past her jaws. But just as quickly as this happened, one of the babies with an embed headlight, shot from its burrow to snap at Carla's heel. It was still grabbing and snapping at her when I arrived to aid her. I swung my hammer dead into the little monster's headlight, with bad intentions. The blow made it release Carla. But oddly, the bigger fish appeared unconcerned with us, as it regurgitated another previously consumed meal towards its brood.

Free at last, Carla managed to position herself on the baby creature's back. Then placing her hands on either side of its back, she quickly nodded towards me to join her, and I did. Once positioned behind her on the baby carnivore, my skin touched hers and I got the scoop. She'd survived the decent by remaining in the air pocket at the roof of the beast's mouth. And she now used her telepathic powers to turn this baby whale "thingy" into an overgrown cab. We broke the surface amazed to be alive.

"Damn, girl! Who in the hell gets swallowed whole by a whale?" The accusation made no sense, but to keep it one hundred, that's never stopped me before.

Still touching Carla, I saw she wanted to say, "Fool, do you think before you speak?"

"Well, as a rule, no." I answered her unspoken question.

On that point, I mean like what's the point thinking before you speak? People say that, but it never made sense to me. Plus, thinking just leads to problems and brain tumors, at least that's what I read on the internet back in the day. I told daddy this once over breakfast. He just looked at me and cursed, "Damn, I knew we should have had a backup kid. Loretta! Call that doctor and see if it's too late to untie your tubes? Quick, 'cause I feel my seeds drying up a little bit more every time I speak to this boy!"

As we dismounted the baby whale thing in the shallow waters of the beach, she responded to my confession, "Don't you realize that not thinking before you speak, is very much the definition of a fool…" Took me years to figure out what my daddy was trying to say. In that moment, I thought that my daddy was there on the beach with us. She must be some kin to my daddy, I thought. No, wait, that wouldn't be good. Damn…

I went on, "I guess so, but not fifteen minutes ago, you were literally knocking boots with this fool."

Placing her index finger on my forehead, "You know what? You're right. I may be the bigger fool."

"May?"

Carla pushed me away and marched off to where our clothes still laid. We were still fussing just a bit as we dressed, when I offered, "Yes, I may be a fool."

"May?" she replied and smiled just a bit.

"But I put it down, huh?"

Carla smiled again. She didn't say a thing, but her body language said all I needed to hear. Finally, she said "Relationships are about much more than sex."

"But it's great start, huh?"

She smiled again, then turned to walk back towards the jeep we'd taken from our captors, talking as she walked, "We're gonna need to find somewhere to set up camp. Maybe setup something simple to keep the rain off of us, while we build a more permanent structure.

Just then it struck me, that we couldn't go back to the City, ever again. Not that I liked living there very much; too much foolishness, even for a fool like me. But I'd gotten used to it, and I knew how to get by, though just barely most of the time.

Carla added, "And our camp needs to be near running water. It's cleaner."

I'm thinking to myself, damn this girl is smart. She didn't realize that her uncle was a scumbag and she didn't know how to untie herself from that chair like I did, but otherwise, she's seems to know everything.

So, we drove along the beach until we ran into a stream. Most of the time we were driving she was talking about the whale being confirmation of something called Interplanetary Evolutionary Convergence across worlds with same climate." and how that thing filled the same role as whales back on Earth. Of course, I knew that all she knew about whales, she got out of some old dusty books. Whereas, I'd seen real whales. They were on the TV, but still I'd actually seen them. Anyway, all of a sudden, she yelled, "Bingo!"

"Huh?"

"I saw that word in your head, when we started, you know, back on the beach. Seems to be one of your favorite words. I've seen it in the heads of a few elders who've I've touched. What does it mean?"

"I don't know if it means anything. But there was a game that old folks used to play back on Earth. When you won you had to scream bingo!"

"Huh…? Anyway, here's a stream running out to the lake. This should do for us to setup."

I found a pair of trees under which I began to setup camp. I dumped some of the bagged-up dope in the back of the truck, and used the huge bags to make a tarp, by melting their edges together. I came up with that myself. I'd hang it from the branches above us the following day I figured. So, we slept that first night in the bed of the truck, since it was enclosed and all.

Well, the next morning, when we stepped out of the truck bed, we were greeted by a couple of tiny flying things, that looked very much like humming birds we had back home.

Carla said. "Evolutionary convergence, again…"

"What the hell is she talking about", I thought to myself again. Anyway, so we're both standing there, when the two hummingbird looking things buzz right up to our faces, changing colors like a kaleidoscope, then in unison, the pair of them move back away from us. But as they did, other little birds of the same feather join them. Not just a couple, but hundreds of them came from all over the lush canopy. They swirled and then took form. Not just any form, but the form of a human face. Perhaps we should have run, but it was just as beautiful as it was scary. Then we heard guttural sounds coming from the flock of tiny birds. Then I realized that it was saying the same thing over and over, but somehow tuning its annunciation with each try. At last I understood what it was trying to say, "Evolution convert. Evolutionary conversion…" Then for several heartbeats it stopped speaking as the birds shifted to and from through several facial expressions. At last, it said. "Hello."

"Hello, my name is Carla and he's John. What is your name?"

"We are all there is, so we have no need of a name."

"Oh…" I said, as what it said did make sense in a way, to me at least.

Then the collage, or whatever you call it, spoke again "Why are you here?"

Carla answered, "Well, there are some very bad people who want to hurt us where we used to live. So, we decided to come here to live."

The birds buzzed some more, then stated "Well, if you stay here, it's unlikely that you will live for very much longer."

"Hmmff…" I said in my Scooby Doo voice.

Dropping her head, realizing what was happening well before I did, Carla asked, "How many?"

"Three trucks similar to yours, with five like you in each one."

As she pondered, Carla said out loud, "Two against fifteen. Not great odds." Then she added, "Where are they now?"

The fluttering face answered, "Right behind you, coming down the beach."

We both turned to see the three damn trucks rolling through the sand towards our location. Carla and I grabbed out weapons out of the truck and took positions behind it.

But then the face asked, "Do you want to play a game?"

"A game?" Carla asked looking back at the face in confusion.

"Yes, a game. Or better said, a contest between you and your opponent. The winner goes free and the loser we eat for lunch."

The word, "What?" flew out of my mouth.

The face, then repeated itself, "Yes, the winner goes free, and the loser shall serve as our meal for the day."

Given the odds, and seeing those fools jumping out of their three trucks we both nodded in agreement. We placed our guns against the truck next to us, just in case this did turn into a gun fight.

After we agreed, the face flew over to our pursuers, to offer the game to them as well. But before the face could even say a word, several of the men opened fire on the floating face. The face responded, even as several small birds in their collective fell dead to the sand by swarming one of the armed men, eviscerating him in a matter of seconds, leaving only his crumpled skeleton where he once stood.

"Damn…" I uttered.

Then the face reformed and again began to speak to the now fourteen armed men, "We'd like to play a game…." Them jokers bobbed all of their heads yes, before the face even finished speaking.

The face smiled and said "Bingo!"

Carla looked at me as I shrugged my shoulders, once more.

The face turned to Carla and suggested, "Since you were here first, Carla, you pick the contest."

Carla was silent for a moment, but then smiled before answering, "Okay, do you guys see that island out there, with a few trees on it?"

The men all nodded.

"If any one of you reaches the island before either us, you win. But if either of us gets there first, we win. Real simple.

The face smiled again, "Then it's settled, we have our contest!"

The men stripped down to their briefs and we did the same. But once Carla got down to her panties and bra, I noticed them fools checking her out, so I repositioned myself between them and Carla as we moved towards the water's edge. While we strolled along and I was hyping myself up, Carla touched me slightly and in doing so, passed a thought into my head. "Follow my lead, she said."

I whispered back to her, trying to be sly with it, "I got this?"

"Slow your roll cowboy…" She said, though it was clear to me by then, that she said a lot of things, that she'd seen in old movies at the library. "Trust me."

Well, as y'all know by now, I'm a take charge kind of guy. But fourteen to one, weren't the best odds, I thought.

Carla still holding my hand, replied back, "I can hear what you're thinking! Fourteen to one, my ass. Just keep up sledgehammer…"

As all sixteen of us lined the beach, the face offered, "This is so exciting!!!" It continued, "We'll countdown to the start. Three, two, one, go!"

So, off we all went. Carla was hauling ass, literally. Sorry, seeing her in her panties set me off, regardless of how close to death we might have been. I can't help myself. So, anyway, Carla wasn't kidding, I did indeed have trouble keeping up with her. I wasn't sure if anyone could keep up that kind of pace for the mile or so to the island.

Then all of a sudden, Carla dove beneath the waves. Startled, I swung up awkwardly with my next couple of strokes, before regaining my focus. Even swimming full out to keep up with Carla, I saw as least two of the other guys out in front of me.

Then just as suddenly as Carla had disappeared beneath the waves, she reappeared riding on top of one of those whale things. She'd managed to link minds with the damn thing. They slowed enough for me to climb on, then off we took for the island. Sure, the guys sent to kill us would say, that we cheated, but no rules were ever stated. Besides, they all knew the mission to kill us, was a one-way mission. No one comes back from the Lush. The face was there on the island when we made landfall. The face smiled and called out, "Bingo!"

Bingo, indeed.

Epilogue: Believe it or not, we were able to survive out there for quite a while, by using Carla's gift and my strong right arm (though mostly because Carla being able to communicate with the creatures made them less likely to eat us, funny how that works). And perhaps more amazingly, I was faithful the whole time, and not just because Carla could see my every thought with just a touch. No, it was more the case, that there weren't really a lot of options out there in the Lush. What can I say...? I told y'all I was a fool.

Particles

"Bullshit! Complete and utter bullshit!" I yelled.

Nahara laughed, "Lucian, that's what you get when you use an open source A.I.!"

"Yeah, but it was free, you know?"

"But in the end, was it though...? Now you've got to spend your whole day trying debug that mother."

"You're right. Seems as if there's a hard way to do something, I'm going to find it, come hell or high water."

"So, it seems..." Nahara replied, as she reviewed our charts. "Just remember, we need to be ready by noon, ship time tomorrow to make our jump window. Otherwise, we might wind up in the hole on this deal."

"Oh, I'm well aware of that. We can't afford to go negative on this thing. And just for the record, if I had known that we'd actually get this contract, I would have just paid for the proprietary AI software."

"Typical startup woes. By the way, just how well do you know these folks?"

"Oh, I don't know them at all. But they paid the deposit, and they put the balance into our One United escrow account."

"They must really like you..."

"I guess so. Anyway, the bank holds the money until both sides are satisfied. What could go wrong?"

"Should I count the ways?"

"No, not really. But you're going to do it anyway, aren't you?"

"You know I could, and probably should, but I won't. You know why?"

"No…"

"Because, I'm too focused on what I have to do, to be worrying about stuff you're supposed to be handling."

"I'm on it." I paused for a moment, and after nodding towards her personal area, I inquired. "When we worked at corporate you always traveled light, but I noticed that you loaded a couple of extra crates this time…?"

"And…?"

"What's in them?"

"Personal stuff."

"Well… do you want to tell me, what kind of personal stuff?"

"Boundaries!" she yelled, before softening a bit, "but no, not really…"

"Girl, you know you, tripping now, right?"

"I had a dream."

"Really, what was it?"

Nahara just smiled at me and continued through her pre-departure systems checklist. I stood there, waiting for some sort of real answer, while she kept on working. Finally, I gave up, sat back down and spun around towards my screen, scanning for bug fixes for our AI. But as I did, I yelled over my shoulder, "Forget you then…"

Nahara offered no reply, beyond to continue hammering on her keyboard, with her back towards me.

So, the next day arrived and with only an hour left to make our jump window, the AI was still freezing up during its simulation exercises.

Nahara spun around in her seat towards me and shouted "Shut that thing down! I'll be our navigator. Unlike some, I actually went to school and got a degree in starship navigation."

"So, what are you trying to say?"

"Oh, I said what I said. See in this thing they call college, some of these degree programs actually do try to teach you how to do something, should say, your A.I. go belly up, halfway across the universe."

"Wow, I didn't know you could do that."

Nahara just stared at me, saying nothing.

"Okay, I knew that you got your degree in it, but I didn't…"

Spinning back to her workstation, Nahara yelled, "Women like me, were navigating the stars long before I came along. So just sit down and strap in, before we miss this window! As it is, we're going to need to slingshot around a couple neutron stars." Then as she turned to face her monitor, the bionic contact lens in her left eye engaged the onboard navigation system, and with just a thought, and an audible command for confirmation, "Engage", our space craft ascended from its Mars orbit.

"Engage?" Curious of her word choice, I inquired, "Why do you say that?"

"Boy, that's from some old creative content, long before either of us was born." Nahara paused for a moment, before going on. "Lucian, let me ask you something?"

"Sure."

"How do you identify?"

"What do you mean?"

"Black, white, other?"

"Oh, I see. You want me to pick a team."

"Well, when you're with me, you definitely present as black. But I'm just curious about how you are when I'm not around? Your curly hair, your complexion, I'm just saying that in certain spaces, you definitely have options."

"Honestly, I don't even think about it."

"Hmm, no shade intended, but that pretty much answers my question."

"Really?"

"Because when you're black or identify as black, you can't help but think about it. One may not think about it when they're home, within a black household, but otherwise, pretty much yes, it's a constant awareness. Our blackness is the one constant we take into every equation. From the moment of our birth, it is cast upon us, and documented as such. It's been that way for over six hundred years now. And just so you know, two hundred years ago, you would have been called biracial and four hundred years ago you would have been mulatto, and unable to vote or own property anywhere outside of maybe New Orleans."

"Damn, girl."

"Damn, indeed."

A moment passed and I asked, "So, I heard you mention something about a neutron star?"

"Yeah, to make sure that we get to where we're going before our contract expires, we're going to need to boost our speed."

"But isn't that dangerous?"

"It can be, but no more so than the whole concept of traveling to the other side of the galaxy."

I nodded, "Well, yeah, when you put it that way."

Five days later in our spacetime bending exercise towards our destination, we neared the first of two neutron stars we'd leverage to make our deadline. Opening our observation window, we stood in amazement at what our eyes beheld. The added stress upon our craft caused the vessel to creak and moan, as our velocity accelerated. Once we cleared the behemoth, Nahara and I both released sighs of relief.

Returning to her seat and then after confirming our increased speed, Nahara announced, "One down, one to go."

"When's the next one?" I asked

"Three days ship time. I'll start staging for that one tomorrow."

"Got it. Hey, since we have a minute, can I ask you a question?"

"Sure…"

"I know why I'm here. I like money and the margins on these deals are amazing. But why are you here? I mean, yeah, we worked together for years, and I know that others from the firm who went independent before me, reached out to you. But you turned them all down. And yet, here you are. What's the deal?"

"You're right. I've done this very same thing for the firm for years. But the risk versus reward of doing it on my own never made sense for me. The financing terms on the front end offered to me, were never as good as what others got. And the others from work, who approached me to join them, never wanted to make me an equal partner. They either wanted to pay me like a month's pay or at best a five percent share. My life is worth more than that."

I paused for a moment, taking in what she was really saying. Shaking my head, I offered, "I'm sorry."

"Thanks, but don't be. You going fifty, fifty with me, is all I could ever ask of anyone." She stopped for a moment, before pulling back another layer, "…and the haul from this one trip, could not only help those in my family, who haven't done as well as me. And dare I say, perhaps this will tilt us towards some sense of generational wealth. Hell, a couple more of these, and we might even be able to start our own settlement on Mars, Europa, Titan or even one of those super earths. This one trip could very well set me on the path towards changing the lives of the ones I love. So, that's why I'm here."

"Understood…" I offered softly.

"Plus, honestly when the dust settled and I found out where we were going, I got a bit pumped. I've heard that their leader is a seer. I'm hoping to chat with some of the locals to find out more about her." I didn't recall that I'd ever seen Nahara so excited about anything.

Nahara sharing so much of herself with me, moved me to share something more of myself as well. "Nahara, yes looking as I do, I get a pass, so to speak, from what you and your family have had to deal with. Though, let me share this. My mother's mother, is clearly bi-racial, and identifies as a person of color. Right before I graduated from undergrad, she explained to me, that the sense that I could do anything, at my very core, was the center piece of the privilege I enjoyed. But she explained that people of color often operate from a sense of lack. 'And though that societal prison is hard to escape from, the mental prison that comes with it, can be impregnable.' She told me to treat everyone the same, and to be intentional when I encountered opportunities to level the playing field. I guess that even then, she could see where my life was going."

"She most certainly did." Nahara replied.

A couple of days passed as Nahara prepared for our second neutron star encounter. And actually, this one would actually be a Pulsar, so it would be a little trickier, or so Nahara tried to explain to me. I just nodded my head to everything thing she said. Mostly, I just listened for any detail that might impact our ability to meet our deadline.

And in case anyone is wondering, no I didn't try to holler at her during the trip. And not that I didn't find her attractive, I did. In fact, before I got promoted into management back at our old firm, I asked her out a couple of times (which she declined). But once I was got my promotion, I moved on from even thinking about doing such a thing at work. We had a strict policy regarding managers dating line staff, and being, as I mentioned before, about my money, I moved on. But that being said, this woman literally held my life in her hands, so I wasn't hardly going to do anything like that, which might take her off her game. And in a closed space like that, that would be the absolute creepiest thing to do.

As we approached the Pulsar, a light began to blink on the navigation control panel, causing Nahara to return to her seat. "Hmm…"

"What?"

"There's a bit of an anomaly, in the pulsar's orbital rotation. Plus, there are several mini black holes that we didn't know about, orbiting it as well."

"Can you handle it?"

"Don't I always?" Nahara took manual control of our ship as it began to creak once more, "I'm overriding the navigational system until we're through this. So, buckle up. Needless to say, we'll want to avoid these little black holes."

"Should I be worried?"

"Big picture, no. I mean from a quantum perspective, there's speculation regarding the future state of one's reality when encountering large gravitational sources like these. But it's so hard to test, given that we're only aware of the reality that we experience in any given moment. It's like some grand double slit experiment."

"Huh, what does that even mean?"

"Right now, it means leave me alone, so I can work."

Less than an hour later, we were clear of the pulsar and all the bodies orbiting it. Nahara announced, "We should be good now."

"Great!" I offered.

"Yes, indeed. But I need some shut eye now. I've set alarms for any anomalies that might need to be handled."

"Anomalies? Handled? What?"

"Like if a star in our path goes nova, or another spacecraft is bending spacetime too close to us."

"What? I don't know anything about that stuff!"

"Oh, I know. All you have to do is wake me if that red light over the navigation system starts flashing on and off. Got it!"

"Got it."

Having not slept in at least two days, she slept hard for a good eight to nine hours. Nahara was straight up and super nice, inside and out. Although she wasn't what I would have called fun. But as she slept there in her bunk with her privacy curtain pulled shut and head turned towards the wall, as to not be disturbed by the flashing lights of the ship, it occurred to me, that maybe the Nahara I'd seen all those years at work might not have been the real Nahara? I mean, if she felt this need to be on guard all the time, this need to be perfect and non-threatening, how could she have ever let her hair down and just be. This trip meant so much to her. Meaning that it is about more than just money for her, it was in some ways also about another level of freedom, which she'd never known.

As for me, while I'm not personally wealthy, my family is, so I knew that there would be other opportunities, should this mission fall through. And yes, there is a family trust so that no child of my grandparents should ever be out on the street. Thus,

I realized that this, all of it, was merely a scorecard for me. I wasn't sure what that should mean to me, but something within me said that it should mean something.

Two weeks later, ship time, as we neared out destination's star system, we began the process of coming out of hyperspace. I was in charge of the cargo. And just what is it that I'm carrying that would justify a trip across the Milky-Way? Well, let's just say that the variation in the generation of stars and the systems which orbit them, means that every star system is richer in certain elements than others. Consider that there are entire planets made of diamonds and others made of entirely of precious metals. In this instance, our buyer's world was poor in certain elements and isotopes commonly found on Earth and Mars. But their world was rich in several elements which are rarer on earth, such as gold. And there is the rub. With the advancements in space travel, when it came to minerals, shipping costs were down to five percent of total costs and falling. The real cost of obtaining any desired element, was mostly the cost of extraction. Thus, you could literally order minerals from the other side of the galaxy at a lower cost than excavating the same substance from one of your outer planets. In business, this is called an arbitrage, or what is simply in layman terms, as a hell of an opportunity. Once you pay off your hauler, it's cash city, for decade upon decade.

Our client's planet was called "Nnwere Onwe", pronounced, "Ounnwayray Onway." As we entered their shipping lane, we announced ourselves using the protocol and translation schema provided from the Earth's global state department. "Hello, this is the USS Particle. We are a cargo vessel with goods to deliver. We are transmitting our purchase order and invoicing details simultaneously to this hailing feed. Please confirm that you are receiving this transmission." This was nothing, Nahara and I hadn't been through before on behalf of our corporate employer in the past, but it was different this time, as it was only the two of us, and we were speaking with our own voices, on behalf of our own selves. There was a difference. These weeks with Nahara had shown me that.

Nahara navigated us over to our assigned orbiting warehouse, where we were to offload our cargo and pick up an entire cargo bay of gold and platinum. All proceeded pretty much as it had before when we'd done much the same for corporate, except that we got a special request from the buyer. They wanted to meet us, in person. Nahara and I looked at one another, shrugged and both said "Sure."

We exited our craft and entered the warehouse. Life on this world was carbon based like our own, but with a richer mix of oxygen, thus Nahara and I wore a very light environmental modulator versus a full-on air tank, which filtered about a third of oxygen in their air. We both had language plugs in our ears, to make communicating fairly seamless.

Nahara and I sat in the common waiting area setup to accommodate earthlings like us, while our vessel was off loaded and as, in our case, loaded with product to take back with us. But as we sat, I got an update on my communicator that our payment had been released, but there was also a note attached which stated that our buyer wanted to meet with us, in the private conference room reserved for the big shots and big shot conversations. In all honesty, the two of us, were basically just noobs, making their first big mark. But we acquiesced, if only to see this room, which we'd only heard whispers of, even when we worked for corporate. Thus, we accepted their offer, and were ready and eager to be upgraded.

When we reached the room, we stood in awe, as the doors to the room swung open before us. Let me say that this room was lined with gold and other precious minerals. Nahara, the walking encyclopedia, could only say "Wow!".

Through convergent evolution, these were bilateral beings, who were largely humanoid in appearance, except that they were all giants, standing ten to fifteen feet tall each. All of the workers, including the one that escorted us to the big boy conference room, were so very regal in hues from coal black to caramel.

The greater percentage of oxygen in their atmosphere supported their larger size, and most of the oxygen dependent creatures in their world were gargantuan when compared to creatures on earth occupying similar places in our respective ecosystems. Another benefit to so much oxygen, was that it discouraged unwanted guests, since it's so reactive. In fact, for those born into the dominate conditions for sentient life in our galactic cluster, oxygen rich worlds are like huge pits of acidic vapor.

 Moments later our hosts, each regally adorned, took up their positions around the table. They sat with their legs crossed, such that their elbows could rest on their knees. You could tell by their attire, that they were in a royal class of their own. After making introductions all around, our hosts made it plain, why'd they'd sought an audience with us. Taking the talking stick into her hand, their leader began to speak. "It has come to our attention, through our emissaries to your world, of the conditions in which black and brown people are forced to live." She stopped for a moment and then looked directly towards Nahara, "Thus, I have discussed with our governing body the possibility of relocating all of you who desire to do so, here, to live on our world. Our poles are cold to us, but temperate by your standards. Or if you collectively desire your own world, we have, what you might call, terraformed, the next planet out from our world. Life developed much later on it, so even now, it's simply a world only of vegetation and lower-class organisms. We as a people, have decided to offer either option as a sanctuary to you, my sister."

Nahara sat still for a heartbeat, and even before she answered, I could see the ice melting within her "Your offer is the most wonderful thing…" Then she sniffed a bit before going on. "You don't know what this would mean… We're all… just… so tired…" And at that she began to openly weep.

And while she wept as our hosts looked on in apparent puzzlement, I dared to inject, as I placed a hand on her shoulder seeking to comfort her. "She's crying, because she's simply overwhelmed by your offer."

The queen responded, "Our Creator has made us such, that we might intercede on behalf of one of her own, in a time such as this. Thus, that is what we will do. We will offer free passage to all who wish to come. Is this acceptable to you?"

Still unable to speak, Nahara, nodded.

For the record, I spoke up for Nahara, "That's a yes."

Finding her voice, Nahara added through her tears, "Yes, on behalf of my brothers and sisters back home, I accept your offer. There are so many thoughts rushing through my head, regarding what needs to be known and what needs to be done, to accomplish this. If you can assist in repairing our AI unit, perhaps Lucian can return home, while I gather the details of your offer, and together we can work through a first draft of the logistics involved."

Something within me, that thing that had moved in me as we reached our destination, would not be silent any longer, "No, if you will allow Nahara, I'd like to stay here with you, to get this going. When we created this business, we tied our fates together, come what may."

"What about the cargo they're loading onto our ship?"

"It's not going anywhere. We'll undock and put our ship into a high orbit, until we're ready to go back." I paused for a moment, placing my hand on her forearm, "Nahara, you're the most capable person I've ever known. You always figure it out. And with my network you'll have access to the right ears to get this rolling. Not to mention whatever assistance our hosts here may provide."

Their leader spoke to Nahara's concerns. "Yes, do not worry, my friend, we will be here. The Creator has already shown us that this will be. We've already identified several large cargo vessels suitable to be converted into arks. My number two will work with you in this matter. But I am never far away, if you need me. Lastly, learn to trust in your gifts, young sister."

In that moment just as our host were about to leave, Nahara's eyes opened wide and she remembered what she'd brought along for journey. "Just a second, please." She walked over to the two crates she'd had port workers bring from our ship to the conference room. Opening the crates, Nahara pulled out several rolls of Kente cloth, placing them on the table. As she placed roll after roll of colorful cloth on the table she explained. "Here, these are our gifts to you. The woven patterns in each of these tells you where it was made, for the different peoples of Africa sew in their own patterns. I don't know why I brought these, it was just something I dreamed about and was on my heart to do..." Standing there with tears still in her eyes, Nahara held the last roll up to our hosts.

Their leader smiled as she responded without translations. "Ase..."

Before this encounter, I'd never been one to believe in destiny, as most spoke of it. You create your own fate; I was always taught. You create your world, your own universe even. But on that day, and in the days to follow, I realized that fate had chosen us.

In the larger sense the two of us were simply two probability waves, which resolved into this particular brave new future. For the fate of a people rested in the fate of these two particles. May our aim be true.

Entanglement

The Awakening

My dream breaks and I awake with a start. Butt naked, wondering, and wandering? Who's apartment? Who's bed? I've done it again; gotten so wasted, that I can't remember what or how?

Rolling to my right, I see a note on the nightstand. It reads simply, "There are more than 2 of us."

Suddenly, there's a loud banging on the door, and with that snatching of my soul, time flowed once more…. "What the hell?"

I called out, "Hold on, just a second!" I jumped out of the bed, disoriented, as I searched for my clothes, any clothes. But try as I might, all I saw were woman's clothing. Whoever it was, was still banging on the door, "yeah, yeah…!" I yelled. Finally realizing that I just needed to find something, my eyes landed upon a pair of leggings that might halfway fit. Reluctantly, I donned them and headed to the door.

I reached the door, but before I turned the lock, I heard a dude say, "Come on, honey, let me in.", and for a moment time is frozen again.

"Honey???" The word and tone struck me wrong.

To this discord, I responded, "Honey? What? Who are you looking for?"

"Come on Donna, it's me, Raymond. Time to go."
Again, I'm cast into timelessness.

"Raymond? Not my partner Raymond…?" I thought, as confusion ran rampant through my entire being, and my heart began to race. The metal door between us is mildly reflective, and something about my reflection, out of focus as it is, doesn't look right. Stepping back, seeing a full-length mirror in the hallway, I at last get a good look at myself. And there I see it. Rouge on my cheekbones, twists in my hair and dark eyeliner overly applied to my eyelids.

"What the Fuck?" I ask my reflection. That brief moment the silence from the universe is deafening.

The voice through the door calls out, "Hey, look I know you're scared. That is completely and totally understandable. I get that. And if you don't want to go through with it today, we'll just…" The voice pauses, then begins again, "Look buddy, I'm over my skis here, but we'll figure it out. We always do."

"We?" I pose to the universe, and once more there is only silence.

But the voice hears it differently, "Well, yes, *we…* we're all behind you. Hey, I'm just gonna take a seat out here until you're ready to open the door. I can only imagine how hard this must be."

Returning to the flow time again, I turned away from the door and stumbled towards the kitchen for a glass of water. Then, I see it. A calendar taped to the refrigerator door, with a date circled in bright red lipstick, March 15th, 2019. In that moment, I finally realized the sum of things, even without a proper accounting. It had happened again. The last thing I recalled it was in December, 2013 and my wife had just left me. Four months of suffering through a debilitating depression brought on by the death of our first born, was more than she could bear. I returned home days before Christmas to find her gone. All she left was a note, "I can't. I'm sorry." Then in quick order, I came to find out through her family (reluctant though they were to share) that she'd changed her name back, moved across country and asked that I let her be. She felt the need to reassess her life, alone; leaving me to assess my own, in solitude.

Glancing to my right, I took in a stack of papers. The sliver of light arching through the kitchen only teased at the written content. I yielded to the reality of morning, and flipped on the ceiling light. The neatly stacked papers dared me to approach them. Taking a step, I turned the stack to face me. The handwriting resembled mine, with the glaring difference that the author was clearly left-handed.

Right off it was clear that these were intake forms for hospitalization, but it was as though the pages were written in a foreign language. And yet it was as clear as an unwanted diagnosis, that I, *Donna*, was scheduled for gender reassignment surgery that very morning. "What the fuck…", indeed.

Beneath the weight of this new understanding, I collapsed to the floor. Then in a fright, I reached my free hand into the yoga pants I'd thrown on and touched myself with more significance than ever before. I sighed in relief finding things in what I deemed to be their proper order.

Then a thought came to me from seemingly nowhere. I called out to Raymond as tears began to well in my eyes, "Hey man, I'm gonna need a minute here, like quite a few minutes. In fact, there's no telling."

Raymond called back, "Remember, the doctor said that you might get cold feet? All of this is… expected. I'm gonna stop by the precinct for a few, but just call me when you're ready to talk. Okay? We're here for you."

I sat silent. The word "we" hung above my head, but I had no capacity in that moment to process it.

Raymond, continued, "Okay…"

Hearing him through the door gathering himself, I relaxed just a bit knowing him to be gone. Then, I stood up and immediately went to the nightstand next to the bed. I opened the top drawer and stuck my hand in upside down feeing above it. Then I felt it, an envelope taped along the top. I pulled it free and sitting on the bed began to read.

"Dear David, it's Donna, the one mama called the dreamer. And if you're reading this, then things proceeded as I knew they eventually would, and that you're now again the host of this body. I've been hostess of this flesh we both share since November of 2016. When I took possession of this vessel, I was sitting in a pool of blood, not my own, having no idea how I got there. I pray that your awakening was less tumultuous than mine. And yet, I know that these transformations, for us, are only born in chaos."

"I thought for some time, that there were only two of us. But a seemingly random encounter revealed otherwise to me. You're not a murderer, and neither am I. But there is another, whom you do not know, who was somehow involved in the bloody scene into which I was brought back into this world. And it appears by the souvenirs they stashed in our apartment; they've killed often. After researching, I found that the pattern of this serial killer, his method and details of his kills have been found around the world. So, either this person is a part of some demented league, or they are jumping from host to host, as they did with us. Last year, sometime after mother died, they tried to reclaim this host. I barely fought them off. It was then, that I decided to create a paper trail for you, should you ever take possession of this host again. And here you are, reading this now. And don't be too hard on Raymond, he's a good guy. I told him about multiple personality disorder, and it was possible that my other personality, who did not identify as I did, could return at any time. Since you've been in charge since middle school, I never got a chance to express my own desires, until I returned to that bloody scene. But if you are reading this, we are clearly unstable, and I am of the belief that neither of us should ever again enter into a committed relationship, because it's not fair. For, what could either of us actually commit to?"

"I know. It's all too much, and yet, above our drama, the priority is to stop this killer, who can jump from body to body. Admittedly, it seems an impossible task. But there is someone who can help us, someone who can see beyond the grave. I don't have a clue where she is or how you'll find her. But mama always called you the doer and since you're the detective, I trust that you will, because you must. Her name is Halima."

In the Beginning…

So, I'm an asshole, but I was going to die young, so I figured it didn't much matter. My parents told me about my condition and how I wouldn't like make it to twenty-five years old, but it was always abstract. That is until one day, after my annual series of tests, things got real. Seriously, no joke, on a random mid-October day of my sophomore year, days before my twentieth birthday, I was handed a terminal diagnosis along with some ibuprofen (to make the giving up less painful, I suppose). The bad news was capricious and random, just as all bad news is. The addict I shall call "mother" for the purposes of this declaration, stopped to buy me a shake on the way home. I took one sip before slinging it across the burger joint and into the far wall. When breaking the news to me back at the hospital, they told me about the seven stages of grief, but in that moment, it was pointless information, "Why the hell, do I have to move past anger?" In that moment, I decided to do whatever the fuck, I wanted to, everyone else be damned. I was the very definition of "asshole-ry". I'd be dead soon, so what did it matter?

But then a funny thing happened on the way to eternity. The counselor assigned the task of convincing me accept my fate, wanted me to enter hospice, you know, the whole *go home and die thing*. But I wasn't really feeling that. But I was certainly down with the whole *fuck work thing*, so after I withdrew from my classes (I thought I might get the balance of my tuition back for the semester, which would afford me one hell of a sendoff), I went by the lab where I did my work/study. It was a simple job for anyone with half a brain. Basically, all I did two days a week was type up the doc's notes and load them to a SharePoint site to keep his academic and Department of Defense overlords happy enough to keep paying the old fucker.

He was an awful instructor, but apparently, the Defense Department believed his work had enough merit for them to take a flyer on him year after year.

Anywho, his work in quantum physics explored the possibility of being able to transfer consciousness between lab rats. Such things have been looked at before, but only on a purely chemical level.

But this prof was seriously on some next level shit. Since it had been proven in mammals that memories could somehow be passed down from one generation to the next via the mother's RNA (lab rats, inherit the ability to solve mazes that they'd never seen before, that their mothers in a previous life had solved). The implication being that it might be possible to at the very least pass to another person memories and maybe even abilities, like being able to play music, with an injection. So, there was this big push in the research community to chemically replicate the phenomenon. But this old ass dude, came up with a method to map subatomic particles, down to which directions they were spinning, then somehow merging MRI laser tech, he could then map them into this special goo he'd devised. It was like a pseudo brain. Dude was actually doing this at a quantum level. Then lastly, he somehow managed to verify that he'd replicated the old brain, in the goo, supposedly...

But on that day, alone in his lab, in that hour, his *supposedly (the wording of his overlords)*, was more than good enough for me. I had mused with the good professor previously about some applications for his work. Where he was thinking about how to restore functionality and memories to people fighting a brain injury or Alzheimer. But even before my prognosis, I had other thoughts, as I'm sure so too did the military brass who were funding his research. But after throwing the milkshake as I did, a willful intent took form from my earlier musings regarding the old man's work.

After the ideal solidified in my head, I actually hesitated. Not something, that I'm known to do. Strong and wrong, is how many saw me in this life, and it wasn't unwarranted. But equally true, since I never cared what others thought or felt, it worked for me. But in the next moment, sitting at the prof's desk, I wrote a quick email to him, it read "Dude, I'm guessing that you heard by now that I'm literally on the clock to checkout from this world. They gave me three months tops. But I'm not ready to go. Your work is revolutionary, and I want to be your Bunker Hill. So, I'm hopping into the brain slicer, and turning it all the way up. I know it will fry my brain, but since I only have one shot at this, and I'm dying anyway, this is my best option. I'm mapping myself into to goo ball number seven. So, please keep the juices flowing into number seven at all costs, until you can find a suitable host to transfer me into. Regards, Adam, your new Favorite Lab Rat."

The old man's schedule was like clockwork, so I knew that I had just over an hour before he'd arrive. For whatever reason, I never suffered the consequences of doubt. So, I moved with a quickness onto the table, plugged in the helmet sized for humans, strapped it on, laid down and flipped the switch in under sixty seconds.

As the world sees it, I died sometime during in that next twenty minutes. But they'd be wrong. Like being in my mother's womb, I can't really speak to my time during my transition. But I can say this, though I could neither hear, see or feel, at some point I became aware.

Over the months the professor sought ways to provide my "goo brain" sensory perception, and rudimentary means for me signal yes or no to his questions. I played along, providing just enough positive evidence for him to keep me plugged in.

But what I didn't share with the old guy, was that in my new form, I could see far more than he ever could, in a hundred lifetimes. Through some consequence of quantum entanglement, I could merge my consciousness with others, so that I could see and experience what they did, most often without them being the wiser. But beyond that for a few very lucky souls, I was entangled enough, to supplant their consciousness with that of my own. I guess it would have been fine with them, had I been a benevolent New Testament God. But unfortunately for them, I was an angry, malevolent God, with a taste or blood and the ability to jump from host to host.

Things were going well, though sadly, for the professor, I soon realized that at some point, I'd need to get rid of him.

Quantum Dreams

It happened again this morning, and again during my second sleep. As I laid there again frozen as events transpired all around me. I heard voices and saw sights. If I'm lying on my back, I hear them and see their faces, but when I'm sleeping on my stomach, I can only hear their voices, which terrifies me all the more. At most, it happens only a couple of times a year, but each time it does, it leaves me shaken, as it did this morning.

In this "dream" I was lying face down, as men and women in uniform walked around me, back and forth discussing what to do. Out the corner of one eye, I could see their feet and lower torsos. While it was hard to tell just how many of them were milling about around me, I could see their high-top black military boots clearly. I heard one of the women ask, "What are we going to do, sarge?"

"Hmm, what do you mean?" He asked.

"Really?" she replied.

"Look private, we're still on mission here. We're here to gather information. And until we've gathered all we can, everything else is secondary."

I heard silence in the room, as all of the walking boots halted for a moment. I imagined that all the faces attached to those black boots were frozen staring at the sergeant, then they began to move again. Back and forth the boots passed pas my peripheral vision, until at last I heard one of the privates announce, "Sarge, I think we have it all."

"Good. Let's roll." He replied.

The woman I'd heard earlier asked, "And now that we're done, what about him?"

"What about him? So, you're going to tell me that bullshit we tell the public about how we no longer use *enhanced interrogation techniques*?"

"But, respectfully sir, he didn't give us anything." she said.

"Well, that was his choice."

"Or maybe, he really didn't know anything…"

"Cost of doing business, private."

It was only then, that I realized, at long last, the source and nature of these extremely vivid waking dreams that are visited upon me. Hard as it was to believe, they appeared to be the last thoughts of the dying. I was seeing and hearing what their detainee did as he lay there dying. I don't know how, but somehow, I'm connected to these people, through some sort of collective consciousness that crossed time and space during their final moments. But I can't understand how something like this could pass through me?

…and yet, as someone who believes that nothing in the universe is without purpose, I knew that all would be revealed someday. And while I didn't know the day nor the hour, I knew with certainty, that the day of revelation was coming. For I am as patient as my name suggests. I am Halima.

The March

Some will be arms & legs, moving us forward
Some will be thoughts giving direction
Some will be hearts, offering faithfulness
Some will be souls, keeping us on the righteous path, lest we fall
prey to hate.
Some will be eyes offering visions to inspire us when we get
weary.
Some will be ears listening to foes and friends alike, that we
might know what awaits us.
Some will be tongues, speaking hope into us, in those moments
when we lose faith.
Some will be the names and faces who remind us why we
struggle
Some will be the spirit of our ancestors who live on through us.
Some will be the breath within us, offering just a nod or a smile,
when we feel we cannot breathe.

Ase...

Fallen Angels

Year: 2243

I am the Alchemist. This is why they call me. This is who I am.

I was in the midst of a waking dream, navigating the dream of another, when the siren brought me back to the present consciousness. I heard my cousin Darnell over the loudspeakers, "We have a level one incursion. I repeat, we have a level one incursion. All Jump team members please report to the launch room immediately!"

I was dressed and out of my room in less than a minute.

Our worldwide observation system, which some might call latter day cloud sitting, had detected an incursion. A powerful being from our off-world watch list had just arrived on earth. While others like us typically battled demons, who sought life in the realm of flesh and blood, my family, known as "House of Sacrifice", also had the responsibility of providing protection from hostile aliens; many of whom had in the past propped themselves up as gods to the ancients. I arrived in the launch room first and asked Darnell, "What's up?"

"Take a look." Darnell replied, as he began gathering items for the flight. "Akina just teleported there to do some recon. I'm going out to the ship to prep it. Bring the others when they arrive."

Just as Darnell exited, my daughter Rachel entered the room.

"Who?" Rachel asked quickly as she continued to fasten her garb.

"Nemesis and an unidentified companion." I replied.

"So, the chickens have come home to roost, eh?" Rachel sighed.

"Yes, they have." I answered.

Present that day were, Rachel (ageless warrior with a special suit of armor), my cousins Darnell (all around hero), Reggie (indestructible strong man), Akina (the Time & Space Walker), Kim (electromagnetic powers), Nick my oldest (could transmute the state of any molecule) and Elizabeth (fire starter), Nick's childhood friend from the academy.

Nemesis was the Greek goddess of vengeance. She existed not to protect the Olympians, but rather to avenge them, should they ever fall. It was her sole reason for being. Her presence was concerning, but not totally unexpected since the

Aunties were off planet. My mother Sarah and her sisters Cil, Deborah and Ruth had destroyed her home world Olympus, and killed the remaining old gods there, nearly a hundred years ago. However, many of the children and other descendants from these gods were not present and escaped that Armageddon. Thus, whenever the Elders sent the sisters across the universe to eliminate some threat, they'd call some of us home to take up residence in Aunt Ruth's place, Cloud Seven, to watch over the earth in their stead.

A negotiated peace between star faring civilizations had largely protected the earth from the time the old gods were forced from our world by our ancestors, until Poseidon returned in 1981 (he and his cohorts attempted to build an Omni Portal on earth, which would have resulted in our world being overrun with ravenous creatures from every dimension). Breaking this truce cost the sea god his life. As a matter of protocol for the death of a god, Olympus launched a full-scale attack against the earth. The Aunties repelled them and then at the direction of the Elders retaliated by traveling to Olympus, and leaving only once it was dust beneath their feet. The Olympians were not the last civilization to suffer such a penalty, as the Elders decided that a message needed to be sent that would last across the ages. One after another the enemies of earth toppled across the heavens.

The remainder of the team arrived at the control room one by one. Reggie, who was lodging separately down at the lagoon, rode his motorcycle into the control room. When he entered, Nick and Rachel were hovering over my shoulder as I scrolled through data on my monitor. Reggie commented, "Ah, I see that the Wonder Twins are here."

This is what Reggie called them, even though they had no reference for the moniker. Still, it seemed to amuse Reggie every time he said it, so he did. Upon his arrival to Cloud Seven a week before, he'd not ventured from his station at the beach. If you wanted to see him, you had to go to him. I did. My kids did not. Long story.

Nick and Rachel mumbled almost in unison, "Hi, Cousin Reggie."

As Reggie was dismounting his bike, in walked Kim and Elizabeth. One of the two seemed to have gussied up just a bit more than the rest of us. Reggie gave a quick glance towards the red headed Elizabeth, and then back towards Nick, before shaking his head in disbelief. It was obvious to all that they, over the years, had a thing for one another, but circumstances and commitments had prevented them from ever following through. Reggie liked to tease Nick about this fact. Rachel, who had simply affixed a baseball cap atop her head, and I, exchanged glances as well. But our glances were in regards to the fact that the world could be ending, but this child, Elizabeth, took a minute to fix herself up a bit before joining us. Elizabeth was in a relationship at the time, but as Chris Rock used to say back in the day in regards to a woman always wanting to keep her options open, "You never know..."

While boarding our low orbit transport, it was decided that Darnell would pilot and play center field for this mission. Besides the fact that most of Darnell's powers wouldn't kick in until after sunset, it was our way to leave at least one resource just off the battlefield to watch everyone's back. If things happened to go south, Darnell would join the conflict using weaponry built into our craft, or if the battle raged into the night, he could swoop in himself. It was odd for us to engage pretty much every alpha and beta level resource in the compound for a mission; however, Nemesis was a level one threat, and she had backup with her. We hoped that these two were acting alone and that this wasn't part of some larger invasion. Once in the air, it would only take us twenty minutes to arrive at our destination. Akina, who can easily walk across time and space, went ahead of us to assess the situation. Once in the air, Darnell called back to the others from the cockpit, "Akina has eyes on the second threat, you'll see her visual in a second."

Elizabeth gasped, "That's Magni, isn't it?"

Nick confirmed, "Yes, that's him and he has his father's hammer."

At his father's death, the Norse godling had inherited Mjolnir as his birthright. With it, he was just as big a threat as Nemesis. Our hands would be full with these two scions from realms long since dispatched by our aunts, at the direction of the Elders.

Kim shouted back over the din of our thrusters, "I hope Akina can keep them entertained until we arrive." I nodded back to her, knowing that like me, Akina was so very hard to kill.

I noted that both aliens were from star systems starved for the element iron, and thus, Oxygen was no more to them, than Nitrogen is to us humans. So, I started figuring, "Hmm…"

My daughter Rachel tilted her head and asked, "What?"

"Just thinking on something." I said softly, lost in thought.

Once we'd completed discussing our plan, Reggie leaned in towards me and asked, "Hey, Black Jesus," that was what Reggie sometimes called me. He had nicknames for pretty much everyone. "You still doing that manna from heaven thing?"

His reference was to the fact that in my outreach work on other worlds, I did indeed convert commonly found matter into foodstuff that the locals could eat.

"Black Santa, you know that I still do." Black Santa was Reggie's nickname within the team. I asked, "Sure, you don't want to try some?"

"Naw, cuz I'm good. I wonder how anyone eats that stuff." Reggie answered.

"You get hungry enough, and there will be little to wonder about." I replied.

Reggie nodded and then shifted gears asking, "Y'all heard who the new Elder in waiting is, right?"

Kim lifted her head from her tablet, "Another *Immortal*, right?" Immortal within our community referenced those of us who did not age. No one on our team used that term about ourselves, but that term was how many of these individuals referenced themselves.

"Yep," Reggie replied in a resigned manner.

Elizabeth shook her head, "So, that will mean that eleven out of twelve Elders will be ageless. I'm so not cool with that."

It wasn't a rule, but historically, of the twelve elders, it was seldom that more than four of them were ageless. Conventional wisdom, was that "immortals" seem to be more prone to becoming drunk with power.

Nick chimed in, "The reasoning is that having less turnover will result in more consistent policies and practices."

Rachel reflected and nodded, "Well, yeah, I hear that, but..."

I jumped in, "Yes, the point is well taken, but while it may sometimes be uncomfortable, stirring the pot every now and then is healthy."

Reggie put a bow around the conversation, "It smells, don't it cuz?"

As we descended, Nick, as he often did, even when the Aunties were in play, took the lead. Both he and his sister Rachel served as officers in the earth's star fleet, he as captain, and she as a chief medical officer. She'd left the Corp some time ago to start a family, but Nick lived and breathed it just as much as ever. Everyone listened to his instructions, with the exception of the big burly Reggie, who had engaged in far more of these battles than anyone present.

Once Nick finished laying out our final instructions, Reggie crowed, "So, basically, get them, but don't get got."

As we broke through the rain clouds, we saw the two giants in the midst of causing mayhem on an epic scale. Golden skinned, with black twists dangling, Nemesis was busy trying to stabilize a shiny metal contraption as energy arched from the clouds into it. Akina buzzed around her like a gnat, jumping in and out of this level of existence. The device Nemesis held was just as tall as she was, and just as wicked looking.

Elizabeth stood up, "That's a planetary drill! They're trying to destabilize the earth's core. Open up the back, I'm jumping out!"

Darnell did as Elizabeth requested and she flew down to join Akina. Over our communicators, we heard Akina tell her, "I was able to make the feet for that damn thing go bye-bye, but I can't grab a hold of the device itself to teleport it somewhere safe; too much energy."

Nick replied back to Akina, "Stand down Akina. You're too valuable to all concerned."

Nick said this in reference to Akina being the only resource on our team that could instantaneously ferry personnel across the universe. Thus, at the direction of the Elders, she was not to engage in direct combat. But let's just say that following orders, was never really something that Akina exceled at.

The red headed Elizabeth, flew low over Akina giving her a quick smile, before arching back up towards Nemesis, "I think girlfriend here could use a facial, don't you?"

Elizabeth proceeded to unleash a torrent of flames into the face of Nemesis. While the flames startled Nemesis at first, they weren't hot enough to harm her, much less ignite her flesh. But they were distracting enough to cause her to take a moment to adjust. Matter from her head ban descended down her face to form goggles around her eyes. By artificially expanding the electromagnetic range which she could perceive, they literally allowed her to see through the flames, to her tool of destruction.

Nemesis spoke aloud in the universal tongue, "Here to save the day, are you, righteous as you are? I will concede that we are a warlike people with little regard for human life, but so are you. You are no better than us. And now that you carry your destructive ways into the stars, you are no worthier of life than us. Welcome to Armageddon earthlings, we've had our fill!"

As this was happening, Darnell struggled to deposit us near the Magni, but the Norse god, was busy alternating from stoking the raging storm he'd brewed up and striking the ground with Mjolnir. Nemesis had a plan, but Magni simply wanted to smash as much stuff as possible.

Reggie instructed Darnell, "Just pull up and hover above his head and I'll jump out."

Darnell did as he asked and Reggie, along with his trusty club, leapt out of the cargo bay and onto the head of Magni. As Reggie landed, he swung his club down into the Norse god's metal helmet. The impact was such that a low bass clang could be heard across the battlefield, even over the raging storm. The space god swung to and from trying to dislodge Reggie. But the thing with Reggie was that even though he was a big man, who couldn't pass through a doorway without at least turning slightly, he was very agile; extremely so. If any of us cousins could dance on the head of a pin thing, it would be Reggie.

Finally, Magni, grabbed the helmet from his head and tossed it, along with Reggie, into the tree line.

These events allowed Darnell to deposit the rest of us in between the two oversized combatants before returning to the skies once again. But this is where things began to go off plan. As we entered the battlefield, the software inside of Nemesis' head band began to assess those of us just joining the fight. In doing so, it alerted Nemesis, that I Michael, the one and only son of Black Sarah, was present.

Nemesis, paused for a moment in disbelief. In the universal tongue, she called out to Magni, "It is the alchemist, Michael, son of Black Sarah! What better way to avenge to our ancestors than to slay the only child of that devil woman before we destroy the world of her birth!"

Magni's reply of a wide grin needed no translation. He turned toward me and swung Mjolnir into mother earth causing her to split open. The breach shook all of us on the ground.

Akina, who had been standing atop a tall building which overlooked the battlefield, cried over her communicator, "Enough of this!"

"Stand down Akina! You know the deal." Nick barked at Akina. She wanted to grab a hold of these beasts and teleport them somewhere far away, since she could teleport the drill while it was running. The problem was that she had to be tangible to touch them, and like a bug she could be squashed either before she teleported them or after they reached their destination. And since we didn't really know how they breached our defenses to arrive on earth, such a tactic might not buy us anything more than a brief respite. But knowing Akina, we all knew that she was only going to stay on the sidelines but for so long.

After witnessing the two giants marching in my direction, Kim looked over her shoulder towards me and joked, "Hey cuz, they seem excited to see you. Do you owe them money?" She then mounted her metal skateboard and soared into the air to confront Magni.

My kids, Nick and Rachel stood beside me. For me it was a mix of pride and horror. I was pleased on one level that their first instinct was to protect me, but that was absolutely the last thing I would ever want in such a situation. I looked at them feigning puzzlement, before switching from teammate to Dad.

"Hey, y'all need to be over there taking care of that drill while they're focused on me. Now!"

As they ran off, Kim and Magni traded electrical charges, until both realized it was a futile exercise. Kim then focused her efforts on magnetizing Mjolnir in hopes of somehow making it more difficult for him to use it. All manner of metallic matter, such as steel pipes from underground and railcars from the rail yard, flew into the powerful hammer, but none of it seemed to impede Magni's progress.

Reggie re-entered the scene slamming his club into the heel of Magni, causing the giant to spin and swing Mjolnir down upon him. The force of the blow drove Reggie into the ground.

In the meantime, Elizabeth, reached into her bag of tricks repeatedly to stop Nemesis; realizing that the heat of her flame was nowhere near hot enough to stop her, but nothing seemed to work.

I called out to my teammates, "Guys, all of you, back off. Go take that drill out while we have the chance and leave these two to me. Just give me some room."

Sure, that was quite a statement to make given my circumstances, but it was not completely without merit. While I'd seen less combat than any of the others present, and my offensive skills did not compare to some, I played defense with the best of them. I was hard to kill, so very hard to kill. Thus, I welcomed the attempt on my life.

Nemesis, was very powerful in her own right. She had the ability, within certain limits to adapt to any given situation. Marching towards me, she removed her goggles and unleashed a killing glance which caused every living thing around me to immediately wither. This was typically her finishing move; but our book on her stated that she sometimes did this as an opening move. As one who cannot age or deteriorate, it had no effect on me.

Magni took his shot next by calling a barrage of lightning strikes down upon me. The ground smoldered for acres all around me. Smoke rose to the heavens as Magni called on the wind to aid him in examining his handy work. At last in the clearing air they saw me. I smiled at them, and then in the universal language I shouted back angrily at them, "My turn!" I'm certainly not the destructive force that my mother is, but I can do a few things. I touched the ground liquefying it as far out as my two attackers, making the whole area essentially a huge tar pit. Then, just as soon as they splashed in, I changed it into a particular metallic compound to lock them in place. Magni, struggled mightily, even calling down a second round of lightning from the skies. But he could not free himself. Nemesis however was a different matter. At first, she too was trapped, but then I saw it. I saw her glow a blushing hue, just as our research stated she would do when she called upon her adaptive powers. She summoned the ability to change the state of molecules, the same as my son Nick. And in doing so, she changed the prison around her into its gaseous state and flew up into the air and landed next to her compatriot to free him as well. We were back where we started, or so it seemed. The two behemoths stood side by side facing me. But I waited a moment, for the rest of my plan to play out.

The composite I'd frozen them in was relatively harmless to them in its liquid or solid state. But in its gaseous state it binds with Oxygen and subsequently forms a nearly unbreakable material that solidifies when it came into contact with their alien flesh. With a quickness, their own skin became a metallic prison, and even if they managed to transform this new compound into gas or liquid, it would literally rip away their flesh. And by their still being on the relatively cool earth, the substances would simply solidify upon them again. While their artificial respirators continued to supply the molecules they needed to remain alive, they were little more than statues. Their glistening faces were turned towards the setting sun as the winds became gentle once again. It was quite a sight. I turned and began walking towards the prone planetary drill. From a distance, I could see that with a few quick blows the mud-covered Reggie had broken the planetary scalpel into several pieces. My son Nick worked to turn the chunks into a liquid which ran down the giant hole in the ground the drill had created.

Akina, Kim and Elizabeth joined me on the ground as I walked towards the others.

Elizabeth, who'd only been officially reassigned to our team that year, asked, "What now?"

Kim and I both looked off, before Akina answered, "Well, we used to hold intruders like these and negotiate some kind of terms with whomever they belonged to. But the current Elders really don't believe in diplomacy." We were in an age of zero tolerance, as far the Elders were concerned.

Kim asked, "Can't we just leave them like this and move them off world?"

I answered, "Well, their environmental packs should operate for years, but eventually, they'll run down and they'll suffocate."

I was quiet for a moment before I began again. "But now that they're powered down, with a touch, I could take care of this."

Akina touched my arm, "No cousin, let me handle this. I'll take them to the Pit. We can work out a safe way to unfreeze them later."

Given that I was a man of peace, and in fact a missionary serving in the less traveled corners of the universe, my cousins tried their best to protect me from the realities of our role as the protectors of human-kind. In much the same way, in the previous generation, my Aunt Ruth was protected by her sisters from actually taking a life, because she was so tender hearted and found it so very hard to do. By moving them to the "Pit", a place out of time, we were in layman terms, storing them in a place that was something of a purgatory. Releasing them there, they'd have to fight it out with the demons that existed there in the flesh. But these were powerful beings, and that at least provided them a fighting chance. The "humanity" they despised, offered them a reprieve to some degree. Both being self-proclaimed warriors, they might even enjoy it on some level.

At last I reached Rachel, Nick and Reggie. Reggie staring up into the twilight at the frozen space gods, from atop the last chunk of the drill to be cracked, called out, "Good work Cuz. I'm impressed."

I replied with a smile. This is who I am. This is why they call me. I am the Alchemist.